"I'm very resilient, Doctor."

He looked at her for a long mom...
the desire to lose his fing...
sounds like it has a...

She raised her eyes...

"But you're not goin... ...rges
guessed after a beat.

"Not tonight." And then she smiled, adding, "Not
until I know you better."

They had future stamped all over them. It
surprised him to realize that he rather savored the
unspoken implication.

There were no alarms, no warning bells. Instead,
he found himself wondering about the woman
beside him. Wondering and wanting to know
things about her. Wanting to fill in the myriad of
blanks dancing in front of him.

"Something to look forward to," he said to her.
It earned him another smile. One that seemed to
burrow right smack into the middle of his chest.

Dear Reader,

Welcome back to the second installment of THE SONS OF LILY MOREAU. This time we meet outgoing Georges Armand, a hunky fourth-year surgical resident who is both charming and skillful. Georges comes into our heroine's life by being a hero. Literally. He rescues both her and her grandfather from a car accident. Then, if that isn't enough, he performs CPR on her grandfather, whose heart has stopped. He brings Amos's heart around, but nearly stops Vienna's because he seems to be just too good to be true. And that, dear reader, is what makes our heroine just a bit leery and keeps her from falling head over heels for the handsome young surgeon. Getting her to intimately trust him, and discovering that perhaps he has finally met his once-in-a-lifetime woman, is the journey of self-discovery Georges finds himself on. With very satisfying results.

As always, I thank you for reading and I wish you someone to love who loves you back.

Marie Ferrarella

MARIE FERRARELLA

TAMING THE PLAYBOY

Silhouette®

SPECIAL EDITION®

Published by Silhouette Books

America's Publisher of Contemporary Romance

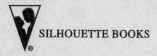

SILHOUETTE BOOKS

ISBN-13: 978-0-373-24856-8
ISBN-10:   0-373-24856-3

TAMING THE PLAYBOY

Copyright © 2007 by Marie Rydzynski-Ferrarella

All rights reserved. Except for use in any review, the reproduction
or utilization of this work in whole or in part in any form by any
electronic, mechanical or other means, now known or hereafter
invented, including xerography, photocopying and recording, or in
any information storage or retrieval system, is forbidden without
the written permission of the editorial office, Silhouette Books,
233 Broadway, New York, NY 10279 U.S.A.

This is a work of fiction. Names, characters, places and incidents are
either the product of the author's imagination or are used fictitiously, and
any resemblance to actual persons, living or dead, business establishments,
events or locales is entirely coincidental.

This edition published by arrangement with Harlequin Books S.A.

® and TM are trademarks of Harlequin Books S.A., used under license.
Trademarks indicated with ® are registered in the United States Patent
and Trademark Office, the Canadian Trade Marks Office and in other
countries.

Visit Silhouette Books at www.eHarlequin.com

Printed in U.S.A.

Books by Marie Ferrarella

Silhouette Special Edition

Her Good Fortune #1665
Because a Husband Is Forever #1671
The Measure of a Man #1706
She's Having a Baby #1713
Her Special Charm #1726
Husbands and Other Strangers #1736
The Prodigal M.D. Returns #1775
Mother in Training #1785
Remodeling the Bachelor #1845
Taming the Playboy #1856

Silhouette Romantic Suspense

In Broad Daylight #1315
Alone in the Dark #1327
Dangerous Disguise #1339
The Heart of a Ruler #1412
The Woman Who Wasn't There #1415
Cavanaugh Witch #1431
Her Lawman on Call #1451
Diagnosis: Danger #1460
My Spy #1472

Harlequin Next

Starting from Scratch #17
Finding Home #45
The Second Time Around #73
Doctor in the House #91

MARIE FERRARELLA

This *USA TODAY* bestselling and RITA® Award-winning author has written over one hundred and fifty novels for Silhouette Books, some under the name Marie Nicole. Her romances are beloved by fans worldwide. Visit her Web site at www.marieferrarella.com.

To
Patience Smith
and
Gail Chasan
who make writing
the pleasure it should be.

Chapter One

The piercing screech of brakes with its accompanying teeth-jarring squeal of tires had Georges Armand tensing, bracing for what he thought was the inevitable impact.

His breath stopped in his lungs.

The unpredictability of life was something that never ceased to amaze him. Given his background and his present vocation, the opposite should have been true.

Georges Armand was the second son of the colorful, exceedingly flamboyant Lily Moreau, a living legend in the art community, both for her talent and her lifestyle. To say that his formative years had been unorthodox was like referring to the Civil War as a slight misunderstanding between two sections of the country. It was true, but a vast understatement. With his mother flittering in and out of his life like warm rays of sporadic sunshine, the one stable thing Georges could always count on was his brother, Philippe Zabelle. The rest of his world seemed to be in constant flux.

A fourth-year medical resident at Blair Memorial, his choice of career, general internal surgeon, also placed him in that same quixotic mix. It was never so clear to him as during his present stint in the hospital's emergency room. One moment, life was quiet, progressing on an even, uneventful keel. Then within the next rotation of the second hand, all hell was breaking loose.

And so it was tonight.

After putting in a double shift at the hospital, rather than electing to sleep for the hours that he was off duty to do his best to recharge his very spent batteries, Georges decided to go out. He was his late father's son and loved to party.

Handsome, with magnetic blue eyes, hair the color of the underside of midnight and a smile that pulled in all living females within a twelve-mile radius, Georges had not experienced a lack of female companionship since the year he turned ten.

From the moment he first opened his eyes twenty-nine years ago, he had been, and continued to be, a lover of women. All women. Tall ones, short ones, rounded, thin, old, young, it didn't matter. To Georges, every breathing woman was beautiful in her own way and each merited his attention.

For a short time.

Of the three brothers, Philippe, three years his senior, and Alain Dulac, three years his junior, Georges was the most like Lily, who, by her own admission had said more than once that she had never met a man she didn't like—at least for a short time.

Tonight he was off to see Diana, a woman he'd met in the E.R. a month ago when she came in complaining of acute gastrointestinal distress. It turned out to be a case of bad sushi. He prescribed medication to help her along and discharged her. And once she wasn't his patient, he dated her. Brunette, brown-eyed, Diana was vivacious, outgoing and said she was definitely not interested in any strings to their relationship. She was the kind of woman you could have a good time with and not have to worry that she was misreading the signs and mentally writing out wedding invitations. In other words, she was perfect.

As he drove his bright red sports car—a gift from Lily on his graduation from medical school—Georges was mentally mapping out the evening that lay ahead. A little dinner, a little dancing and a great deal of romance.

But all that changed in an instant.

The horrifying sound behind him had Georges swerving to the right. The nose of his vehicle climbed up against the hillside embankment. The maneuver was just in time for him to avoid being hit by the vintage blue sedan behind him. The latter was not so lucky. The black Mercedes behind the sedan slammed right into it.

His heart pounding against his rib cage, Georges looked into his rearview mirror. He saw the dark blue sedan spinning around helplessly, like a badly battered pinwheel in the center of a gale. Out of his car in an instant, Georges ran toward the car to see if he could help the passengers.

It wasn't the doctor in him that made Georges bolt out of his barely stilled sports car; it was the Good Samaritan, the instinct that had initially been instilled, fostered and nurtured by his mother. But it was predominantly Philippe who'd taught him that standing on the sidelines, watching, when you could be in the midst of the turmoil, helping, was never a truly viable option. Philippe believed in commitment, and Georges believed in Philippe.

He attributed all his good traits to his older brother, his looks to his mother and his money, of which there was more than a considerable amount, to his late father, Lily Moreau's second husband, Andre. Andre Armand was a self-made millionaire who owed his fortune to the production of a seductive yet affordable perfume. A scent, despite all her money, that Lily still wore.

The instant Georges opened the driver's-side door and was out of his vehicle, he found himself having to flatten his back against it to get out of harm's way. The Mercedes that had rammed into the sedan and had initiated this lethal game of metal tag now whizzed erratically by him. Had he not jumped back, Georges was certain that he would have wound up being the black Mercedes' new hood ornament. Or, if not that, then permanently sealed to the vehicle's shiny grill.

The figure of a dark-haired, middle-aged man registered at the same time that the vehicle zoomed by him. Blessed with incredibly sharp vision and presence of mind, Georges focused on the license plate even as the vehicle disappeared around one of the many curves that typified Southern California's winding Pacific Coast Highway.

The entire incident took place in less than a heartbeat.

Georges was running toward the blue sedan, which had finally stopped spinning. Its front end was now pointed in the opposite direction of the flow of traffic.

The driver's side was mashed against the hillside.

Now that the brakes were no longer screeching and the tires no longer squealing, Georges became aware of another noise, one that had been blocked out by the first two. Screams. The woman within the sedan, in the front passenger seat, was screaming.

Just as he reached the passenger side, Georges saw thin orange-and-yellow tongues of fire began to lick the front of the hood.

From what he could tell, there was only one other occupant in the car, the driver. The gray-haired man was slumped over the steering wheel. Georges tried to open the passenger door, but the impact from the careening Mercedes had wedged the door shut.

Desperate, afraid that any second the engine might explode, Georges tried to break the window with his elbow, swinging as hard as he could. The impact reverberated up and down his arm and shot into his chest, but the window remained a solid barrier.

The woman inside the car looked at him, their eyes meeting as shock pressed itself into her young features. Frantically, she tried to open the window on her side, working the buttons on the armrest. It was useless. There was no power fueling the buttons. The window remained in place, sealing in both her and the unconscious driver.

He needed something solid, such as a tire iron, to break the glass, but there wasn't enough time to run back to his car to get one. Georges knew that the sedan could blow up at any moment.

The Pacific Coast Highway wove its way along the coast with the ocean on one side, a sprawling hillside pockmarked with exceedingly expensive real estate on the other. Searching the ground for something heavy to use, Georges spotted a good-sized rock and quickly picked it up. Hurrying back to the passenger door, he knocked on the window until the woman looked at him again.

"Duck your head," he shouted at her, lifting the rock.

The woman did as she was told, turning her body so that she was shielding the man in the driver's seat. Pulling back his arm, Georges threw the rock as hard as he could at the window. The surface of the glass cracked and splintered in half a dozen places. Wrapping his jacket about his right hand, he punched through the shattered glass and cleared away as much as he could.

"C'mon," he ordered the woman, "You have to get out of there."

The blonde shook her head emphatically. Her arms were still around the old man. "I can't leave him," she cried.

Georges looked from her to the driver. He was old, too old, he judged, to be her husband or even her father. There was blood on the man's forehead and he seemed to be unconscious, but breathing. Georges couldn't be sure of the latter.

He was sure that if he spent time arguing with the blonde, they could all suffer the consequences. Leaning in, Georges grabbed the woman by her waist. Surprised, she began to resist.

"First you, then him," Georges told her firmly. Before she could say anything, he was pulling her through the opening he'd created. He felt the jagged edges scratch at his skin. The blonde weighed next to nothing, even as she struggled against him.

"My grandfather!" she cried as Georges deposited her on the ground.

He examined the other side of the car. It was pressed against the hillside, leaving no room for him. No way could he snake his way in and open the door on that side to get the man out. Without stopping to take into consideration that the car could blow up at any moment, Georges relied on the luck that had seen him through most of his life and crawled in through the window.

The old man's seat belt was still on. Georges hit the release button and pulled the man over toward his side. Moving as quickly as he could, he angled his body so that they could switch places. He needed the old man next to the opened window.

The blonde realized what he was doing. "Push him through," she urged. "I can hold him up."

He had his doubts about that. The blonde didn't look as if she could hold a twenty-pound sack of grain without stumbling beneath its weight. But he had no other option. Putting his shoulder against the man's lower torso, Georges pushed the old man's upper body through the opening.

To his surprise, the woman slipped her arms beneath the old man's arms and moved backward, pulling the deadweight as he pushed him out. He heard her groan and utter a noise that sounded very much like a battle cry.

The next moment, between the two of them, they'd managed to get the old man out of the vehicle.

The second the unconscious driver was clear of the door, Georges dove out, headfirst, tucking down and into his torso just before he hit the ground so that he rolled. In an instant, he was back up on his feet again. Quickly shoving his shoulder down beneath the old man's, he wrapped his arm around the man's waist.

"Run!" he shouted at the blonde.

Instead of dashing before him, the woman mirrored his movements, getting her shoulder beneath the old man's other shoulder so that both he and the old man could get away from the fiery vehicle faster.

Georges thought he heard the old man mumble, "Leave me," but he didn't know if he'd imagined it or not. In any case, he wasn't about to abandon the man, not after all the trouble he'd just gone through to rescue the driver.

They barely made it back to the front of his sports car before the blue sedan burst into flames.

Georges threw his body over the old man and the blonde just as their car exploded. After several moments had elapsed, he pulled back, suddenly aware of another problem. On his knees, Georges felt the man's throat and then his chest for a pulse. There was none.

The blonde stared, wide-eyed, barely holding fear at bay. "What is it?"

In response, Georges threaded his hands together over the man's chest and began to administer CPR. He hardly glanced in her direction, concentrating on only one thing: getting the man's heart to beat again. "I think he's had a heart attack."

"No." The word escaped her lips like a shell being fired, aimed not at Georges as a denial of his statement but at the old man lying on the ground. "No! Grandpa, do you hear me?" She scrambled closer to the man, moving in on his other side. "No, you can't do this," she told him urgently. "You can't have a heart attack."

There was absolutely no response from the driver.

"I don't think he's listening to you," Georges told her in between beats.

Mentally, he counted off compressions, then tilted the man's head back. Pinching his nose, Georges leaned over the man's mouth to blow his breath into it. Once, twice, a third time, before returning to compressions. The man still wasn't responding. Georges didn't allow himself to think about anything except the success of his efforts. Everything else, including the blonde's voice, became a distant blur.

"In my left coat pocket," he told her as he resumed compressions for a third time, "I've got a cell phone." The moment he said it, she galvanized into action, reaching her long, slender fingers into his pocket. He could feel them as they slid in.

As he fought death for possession of the old man's life, it struck him that this was one hell of a way to meet a woman. Because even in the midst of the ongoing turmoil, as he struggled to bring the driver back around, it did not escape Georges that she was one of the most attractive women he had ever seen.

"Got it!" she declared breathlessly, pulling the cell phone out of his pocket. Rocking back on her knees, she began to press the three numbers that popped into everyone's mind during an emergency.

Nine-one-one would generate an appearance of an ambulance driven by EMTs. Given where they were, the paramedics could take them to one of two hospitals, most likely County General since it had a contract with the company that most often appeared on the scene. However, Blair Memorial was just as close as County General and it was the better of the two hospitals. It was also the hospital where he put in his hours.

"Don't call 911," he told her, then rattled off the number she should call before he breathed into her grandfather's mouth.

The blonde looked at him, confused. "Why should I call that number?"

"Because that number will get you the ambulance attendants from Blair Memorial hospital and they have the better emergency room staff," he told her with no hesitation. He spared her a quick glance. "You want the best for him, don't you?"

She didn't bother answering. As far as she was concerned, that was a rhetorical question. So instead, she pressed the buttons on the keypad. Two rings into the call, the receiver was being picked up.

"Blair Memorial, E.R.," a calm, soothing voice said.

Visibly struggling to remain coherent, the blonde clutched the cell phone with both hands as she gave the man on the other end of the line all the necessary details. Finished, she followed up the information with one more instruction.

"Please hurry." With that, she let out a shaky breath and closed the cell phone again.

"I think that's a given," Georges told her.

Her eyes darted back toward the man administering CPR to her larger-than-life grandfather.

Breathe, damn it, Grandpa, breathe! I'm not ready to live in a world without you in it yet. You promised me that you'd never leave me alone. Don't break your promise, Grandpa. Don't break your promise.

Shaking herself free of the terror that threatened to swallow her up whole, she forced herself to look at the man kneeling beside her grandfather. The savior who had come to their rescue.

Replaying his last words, she blinked, trying to focus. "What is?"

"That they'll hurry."

He was sitting back on his heels. A fresh wave of terror drenched her, leaving her shivering. "Why did you stop giving him CPR?" she demanded, an audible tremor in her voice as it rose. The words rushed out of her mouth. "Why aren't you trying to get his heart going?"

He curved his mouth into a slight smile. Triumph at this point, he knew, could be tenuous and very short-lived. By no means was the man on the ground out of the woods. "Because it *is* going," he told her.

Her eyes darted back to her grandfather, searching for proof. Staring at his chest. Was that movement? "On its own?"

Georges nodded. "On its own."

Tears suddenly formed in her eyes. He became aware of them half a beat before the blonde threw her arms around his neck.

Half a beat before she kissed him.

Hard.

Like the oncoming tide, she pulled back as quickly as she had rushed forward. Georges realized that he had tasted not only something sweet when her lips had pressed against his, but something moist, as well. Tears. He'd tasted her tears on her lips. They must have fallen there just as she'd impetuously made contact with his.

They tasted salty and yet, somehow they were oddly sweet, as well.

"Thank you," she cried breathlessly. "Thank you." And then, just like that, her complete attention was focused back on her grandfather. She took the old man's hand in both of hers and held it next to her cheek. With effort, she controlled the tremor in her voice. "Now you just hang on, Grandpa, you hear me? Help's on the way." For a split second, her eyes shifted back to the man who had saved them both.

Georges felt himself getting lost in her smile as she murmured, "Some of it's already here."

Forcing himself to look back at his patient, Georges thought he saw the old man's eyelids flutter, struggling unsuccessfully to open. He took the man's other hand in his and once again felt for a pulse. He found it, albeit a weak one. Mentally, Georges counted off the beats.

The blonde looked at him quizzically, obviously waiting for positive reaffirmation.

"It's still a little reedy," he told her. "When they get him to the hospital, I think your grandfather should stay overnight for observation. They'll take some films, do an angiogram." Georges looked at the man's face. It was remarkably unlined, but he would still place him somewhere in his late sixties, possibly early seventies. Other than the gash on his forehead and the episode he'd just experienced, the man seemed to be in rather good condition. But appearances could be deceiving. "Does your grandfather have any medical conditions that you're aware of?"

The blonde laced her fingers through her grandfather's hand, as if her mere presence could ward off any serious complications. "I'm aware of everything about my grandfather," she told him. There was no defensiveness in her voice, it was simply the way things were. She took an active interest in this man who was very much the center of her world. "He has a minor heart condition—angina," she specified. "And he's also diabetic. Other than that, he's always been healthy."

Georges focused only on what he considered to be liabilities. "Those are complicating factors."

The blonde pushed back a strand of hair that had

fallen into her face. She continued holding her grandfather's hand. "Are you a doctor?"

He smiled. "I'm a fourth-year resident." He thought of John LaSalle, the attending physician that he was currently working under. LaSalle regarded residents as lower life forms only slightly higher than lab rats. "In some eyes, that makes me an 'almost' doctor."

The blonde looked back at her grandfather and, for a moment, watched the way the man's chest rose and fell in grateful silence. She was aware that she might not be watching that if it hadn't been for the efforts of the man beside her.

"There's nothing 'almost' about you," she replied softly.

It took Georges a second to realize that those were not bells he was hearing in his head but the sound of an approaching siren.

Chapter Two

One of the paramedics, Nathan Dooley, a tall, black, muscular attendant who seemed capable of carrying the patient with one hand tied behind his back, recognized Georges the minute the man climbed out of the passenger side of the ambulance's cab. He flashed a wide, infectious grin at him, even as he and his partner, a somber-faced man in his thirties named Howard, swiftly worked in tandem to stabilize the old man.

Doubling back to retrieve the gurney from the back of the vehicle, Nathan returned and raised a quizzical eyebrow in Georges' direction. "What, you don't work enough hours in the E.R., Doc? Going out and trolling the hills for business now?"

"Coincidence," Georges told him, carefully watching the other EMT work. The other man knew it, too, Georges thought, noting the all-but-rigid tension in Howard's shoulders.

"Destiny," Nathan corrected. He was still grinning, but it sounded to Georges as if the paramedic was deadly serious. He moved back as the two attendants transferred the old man onto the gurney and then snapped its legs into place.

His mother believed in destiny. In serendipity and fate, as well as savoring the fruits of all three. As for him, Georges still didn't know what he believed in. Other than luck, of course.

He supposed maybe that was it. Luck. At least, it had been the old man's luck in this case. Georges was fairly certain that if he hadn't been on this road, right at this time, traveling to see his latest— for lack of a better word—love interest, if he'd given in to the weary entreaty of his body, he would have been home in bed right now. Most likely sleeping.

And the old man on the gurney would have been dead. He and his granddaughter would have been trapped in a fiery coffin.

It was satisfying, Georges thought, to make a difference, to have his own existence count for something other than just taking up space. Moments like this brought it all home to him.

Again, he had Philippe to thank for that. Because, left to his own devices, he had to confess he would have been inclined to sit back and just enjoy himself, just as his father had before him, making the rounds on an endless circuit of parties. His father's money had assured him that he could spend the rest of his life in the mindless pursuit of pleasure.

But Philippe had had other plans for him. At the time, he'd thought of Philippe as a humorless bully. God, but he was grateful that Philippe had happened into his life. His and Alain's.

Otherwise, the petite woman beside him would now be just a fading memory instead of very much alive.

"I want to go with him," the blonde was saying to the other attendant, who, as uptight as Nathan was relaxed, clearly acted as if he were in charge of this particular detail.

Her grandfather had already been lifted into the back of the ambulance, his gurney secured for passage. Nathan was just climbing into the vehicle's cab and he nodded at the woman's statement. But Howard was in the back with the old man, and he now moved forward to the edge of the entrance, his thin, uniformed body barring her access.

When she tried to get in anyway, Howard remained where he was and shook his head. "Sorry. Rules."

Reaching for both doors simultaneously, he began to close them on her. But the action was never completed. Coming up from behind her, Georges suddenly clamped his hand down on the door closest to him. It was apparent that Georges was the stronger of the two.

It was also very apparent, especially from the scowl on his face, that Howard did not care for being challenged.

"Let her go with him," Georges told the paramedic. It was an order even though his voice remained even, low-key. "She's been through a lot."

Howard's frown deepened. This was his small kingdom and he was not about to abdicate so easily. "Look, there are rules to follow. Nobody but the patient, that's him, and the attendant, that's me," he said needlessly, his teeth clenched together, "are supposed to be riding back in—"

Georges' smile was the sort envisioned on the lips of a cougar debating whether or not to terminate the life of its captured prey—if cougars could smile.

"Have a heart—" his eyes shifted to the man's name tag "—Howard. Let the lady get into the ambulance with her grandfather."

Nathan twisted around in his seat, looking into the back of the ambulance. "Listen to the man, Howie," he advised with a wide, easy grin. "Someday he could be holding a scalpel over your belly."

It was obvious that Howard didn't care for the image or the veiled threat.

"If you get any flack," Georges promised smoothly, "just refer your supervisor to me. I'll take full responsibility."

"Yeah, easy for you to say," Howard grumbled. Drawing in a breath, he blew it out again, clearly not happy about the situation. Clearly not confident enough to back up his decision. His small black eyes darted from the woman's face to the doctor's. Survival instincts won over being king of the hill. "Okay." Howard backed away from the entrance and returned to his seat beside the gurney. "Get in."

"Thank you," the blonde cried. It wasn't clear if she was addressing her words to Howard or her Good Samaritan, or the man in the front seat behind the steering wheel. Possibly, it was to all three.

Taking her hand, Georges helped the woman get into the back of the ambulance.

But once she was inside, she didn't let go of his hand. She held on more tightly.

"I want you to come, too," she said to him. When it looked as if he was going to demur, she added a heartfelt, "Please?"

There was no more that he could do. The ride to the hospital was fast enough and once there, there would be doctors to see to the man. Besides, he still had a date waiting for him.

Georges began to extricate himself from her. "I—"

Her expression grew more determined. "You said you worked at—Blair Memorial, is it?" Georges nodded. "Then you're one step ahead of everyone else there. You saw what my grandfather went through. You treated him. Please," she entreated. "I don't want to risk losing him. I don't want to look back and think, If only that doctor had been there, that would have made the difference between my grandfather living and—" She couldn't bring herself to finish.

It was the sudden shimmer of tears in her eyes that got him. Got him as surely as if handcuffs had been snapped shut on his wrists. Georges inclined his head, acquiescing.

"I never argue with a beautiful damsel in distress," he told her. Then he glanced up at the frowning Howard who looked like a troll sitting beneath his bridge, protecting his tiny piece of dirt. "Don't worry, I won't crowd you in the ambulance," Georges promised. He jerked his thumb back at his presently less than shiny sports car. "I'll follow behind in my car." Georges shifted his glance toward the woman. "That all right with you?"

Vienna Hollenbeck pressed her lips together to

hold back the sob that materialized in her throat. She was a hairbreadth away from breaking down, and it bothered her. Bothered her because it clashed with the strong self-image she carried around of herself.

Surprise, you're not invulnerable after all.

Nodding, Vienna whispered, "Yes, that'll be fine with me."

Georges gave her hand a warm squeeze before withdrawing his own. "He's going to be all right," he promised.

With a huff, Howard leaned over and shut both doors in his face. Firmly.

Georges turned away and hurried over to his vehicle. Buckling up, he turned the key in the ignition. The car purred to life as if it hadn't come within inches of being crushed.

He'd just broken cardinal rule number one, Georges thought, waiting for the ambulance to pull away. Not the one about doing no harm. That was the official one on the books, the one that was there to make people feel better about going to doctors. He'd broken the practical one, the one that was intended to have doctors safeguarding their practices and their reputations. The one that strictly forbade them to make promises about a patient's future unless they were completely, absolutely certain that what they said could be written in stone and that their words couldn't somehow return to bite them on the part of their anatomy used for sitting.

But he found that he couldn't look into those blue eyes of hers and not give the woman the assurance that she was silently begging for.

"So I made her feel better for a few minutes," Georges murmured out loud to no one in particular. "What harm could it do? Really?"

Besides, from what he could ascertain, the old man didn't look as if he'd sustained extensive bodily injuries.

Appearances can be deceiving.

How many times had he heard that before? How many times had he learned that to be true? The old man could very easily have massive internal injuries that wouldn't come to light until after he'd been subjected to a battery of tests and scans.

Still, Georges argued silently, why make the woman worry? If there was something wrong, there was plenty of time for the man's granddaughter to worry later. And if it turned out that there wasn't anything wrong, why burden her needlessly? He always tried to see things in a positive light. It was an optimism that he had developed over the years and which had its roots in his mother's lifestyle and philosophy: never assume the worst. If it was there, it would find you soon enough without being summoned.

Georges realized that he was gripping the steering wheel a great deal more tightly than necessary. He consciously relaxed his hold. It didn't, however, keep him from squeezing through a yellow light in the process of turning red.

He kept pace with the ambulance, all but tailgating it until it reached Blair Memorial.

The hospital was an impressive structure that was perched at the top of a hill and that seemed, according to some, to be forever under construction. Not the main section, which only underwent moderate renovations every ten to fifteen years, but the outlying regions.

Beginning as a small, five-story building, over the last forty-five years, Blair Memorial Hospital, originally called Harris Memorial, had tripled in size. It owed its name change and its mushrooming growth to generous donations from the Blair family, as well as from myriad other benefactors. None of it would have been possible, however, if not for its glowing reputation, attributed to an outstanding staff.

No one was ever turned away from Blair Memorial's doors and the poorest patient was given the same sort of care as the richest patient: excellent in every way. Its physicians and surgeons thought nothing of volunteering their free time, both at Blair and in outlying regions, rendering services to people who otherwise could not afford to receive the proper medical attention that often meant the difference between life and death, permanent disability and full recovery. Georges was proud to have been accepted at Blair to complete his residency.

The ambulance made a left turn at the light, then an immediate right. Easing around the small space, it backed up to the emergency room's outer doors.

Georges was right behind it. As he brought his car to a stop beside the vehicle, a volunteer valet came to life behind his small podium and quickly hurried over toward the red sports car.

"I'm sorry, I'll have to park that for you in the other lot. We need to keep this clear for emergency vehicles." The words were hardly out of his mouth before he saw the hospital ID that Georges held up for his perusal. The valet flushed. "Oh, sorry, Doctor. I thought you were with them." He nodded at the ambulance. It wasn't unusual for family members to accompany ambulances.

"I am," Georges replied amicably. "There was an accident on PCH. I just happened to be there in time to lend a hand."

Nodding meekly, the valet faded back to his podium.

The back doors of the ambulance were already opened. Georges waited for the gurney to be lowered. Once it was, he offered his hand to the blonde to help her out of the vehicle.

Her fingers were icy, he noted.

"Thank you," she murmured, her eyes meeting his and holding for a long moment.

Georges knew the woman wasn't referring to his helping her out of the ambulance. She was thanking him for coming.

"Part of my job description," he told her.

"Trolling for patients?" she asked, repeating the words that Nathan had used earlier. She tried to force a smile to her lips.

The small, aborted attempt hinted at just how radiant her smile could be once fully projected. He found himself looking forward to seeing it in earnest.

"Helping where I can," he corrected.

The gurney was pushed through the electronic doors that had sprung open to admit it and the attendants. Georges placed his hand to the small of her back, guiding her in behind the gurney.

Warm air came rushing at them, a contrast to the cool night air outside. The next moment, the on-duty E.R. physician was coming toward the paramedics and their patient.

"What have we got?" Alex Murphy asked, pulling on plastic gloves as he approached. The next moment, he stopped, looking at Georges in surprise. The two men had crossed paths a couple of hours ago, with Murphy arriving as Georges was leaving.

"Friend of yours, Dr. Armand?" Murphy assumed.

Georges shook his head. "Hit-and-run," he replied. "Accident happened right behind me on Pacific Coast Highway. Driver of the car never even stopped." He didn't add that he had almost been hit by the same driver. Dramatics were his mother's domain; they'd never interested him. "The man had a cardiac episode. His heart stopped for less than a minute," he added when Murphy looked at him sharply. "I applied CPR."

Georges rattled off the rest of the man's vital signs. When it came to his blood pressure, Georges glanced toward Howard, who supplied the missing piece of information. The paramedic looked annoyed that he had been reduced to the role of a supporting player.

Taking it all in, Murphy nodded. "Okay, we'll take it from here."

Georges felt the woman's eyes on him, as if silently urging him to take the lead. There was no need. Murphy was an excellent physician, but to allay her fears, he turned to the doctor and said, "I'd appreciate it if you did an angiogram on him right away. He has diabetes and a heart condition."

"And this is a stranger, you say?" Murphy glanced from him to the young woman beside him. And then nodded knowingly. "Angiogram it is." Murphy turned toward the nurse and orderly who had taken the two paramedics' places. "You heard Dr. Armand." They began to wheel the old man away, but Murphy stopped them. "I want a full set of films done, as well." He fired the names of the specific scans at them. Finished, he backed away.

The nurse and orderly resumed pushing the gurney down the hall, passing through another set of double doors. The blonde began to follow behind them. Hurrying to catch up, Georges placed a restraining hand on her arm.

Startled, she looked at him, a puzzled expression on her face.

"You can't go there," he told her, then added with a reassuring smile, "Don't worry, they'll bring him back as soon as they're finished."

Murphy stripped off the plastic gloves and crossed his arms before him. "Anything else?" he asked, mildly amused.

Georges nodded. He knew how territorial some doctors could be. It was always best to ask permission rather than assume. "If you don't mind, I'd like to hang around."

Murphy glanced at the woman, who in turn was looking down the hall. Georges Armand's reputation had made the rounds and he, like everyone else, was well aware that the young surgical resident attracted women like a high-powered magnet attracted iron. "Hang all you want, Georges." He smiled wistfully. Married five years, his own romancing days were well in his past. "I'll keep you apprised," he promised.

Murphy addressed the words toward the young

woman, as well, but for the moment, she seemed oblivious. With a shrug, the physician left to attend to the next patient on his list.

"Thanks. I appreciate that," Georges called after him. Turning toward the blonde, he caught himself thinking that she seemed a little shaky on her feet. Small wonder, considering that she'd been in the accident, too.

"You know," he began, moving her over to one side as another gurney, this time from one of the E.R. stalls, was pushed past them by two orderlies, "you really should get checked out, as well."

If she stopped moving, Vienna thought, she was going to collapse. Like one of those cartoon characters that only plummeted down the ravine if they acknowledged that there was no ground beneath their feet.

She shook her head. "I'm fine. Just shaken. And worried," she added with a suppressed sigh, looking over toward the double doors where her grandfather had disappeared.

"In that case, maybe we should get your mind on other things." He saw her eyebrows draw together in silent query. "There's an anxious administrative assistant over at Registration eager to take down a lot of information about your grandfather. Here." He offered her his arm. "I can take you over to the Registration desk so you can talk to her."

Vienna nodded, feeling as if she was slipping into a surreal dreamlike state. She threaded her arm through his in what seemed like slow motion, and allowed herself to be directed through yet another set of swinging double doors.

She tried desperately to clear the fog that was descending over her head. "You know," she said, turning to look at the doctor, "I don't even know your name." The other doctor had called him by something, but she hadn't heard the man clearly. "What do I call you?" She smiled softly. "Besides an angel?"

He laughed then, thinking of what several women might have to say about that. He also caught himself thinking that he'd been right. When she smiled, it was a beautiful sight to behold. "I don't think anyone's ever accused me of being one of those."

"Well, you are," she told him. "I don't…I don't know what…I would have done if…you hadn't stopped to help." Tears stole her breath, blocking her words.

"Don't go there," he told her. "There's no point in thinking about the worst if you don't have to." He stopped walking and gave her a small, formal bow, the way he used to at his mother's behest when he was a small boy. "My name is Georges—with an *S*—Armand."

She shook his hand. "Well, Georges with an *S*, I won't think about the worst but only because I know you saved me from it. Saved my grandfather from it." She paused to take a deep breath. She wasn't going to cry, she wasn't. Tears were for the weak and she was strong. She *had* to be strong. "My name is Vienna," she told him, putting out her hand, "Vienna Hollenbeck."

Her skin felt colder than the last time, Georges thought. "Vienna? Like the city?"

"Like the city." The smile on her lips was just too much of an effort to retain. It melted as she felt herself turning a ghostly shade of pale. Perspiration suddenly rimmed her forehead and scalp. "Would you—would you mind if we postponed seeing the administrative assistant for a minute?"

"Sure. Are you all right?"

His voice was coming to her from an increasing distance. Vienna felt her knees softening to the consistency of custard. The deep baritone voice had nothing to do with it.

"I'm not… I don't think…"

She didn't get a chance to finish. Rather than sit down the way she'd wanted to, Vienna felt herself dissolving into nothingness as the world around her became smaller and smaller until it had shrunk down to the size of a pinhole.

And then disappeared altogether.

Just before it did, she thought she heard the doctor calling to her, but she couldn't be sure. And she definitely couldn't answer because her lips no longer had the strength to move.

The darkness that found her was far too oppressive to allow her to say a word. With a last rally of strength, she tried to struggle against it, to keep it at bay.

But in the end, all she could do was surrender.

Chapter Three

Georges managed to catch her just before her body hit the floor.

Scooping Vienna up in his arms, he looked around the immediate area for an open bed. He saw the nurse and the bed at the same time.

"Jill," he called out to a heavyset woman he'd met during his first day at the E.R., "I'm putting this woman into bed number seven."

Mother of four boys, grandmother of seven more, Jill Foster liked to think of herself as the earth mother of the E.R. night shift. Pulling her eyebrows together, she looked at the unconscious woman he was holding and gave him a penetrating, no-nonsense look.

"Getting a little brazen with our conquests, aren't we, Dr. Armand?"

They had an easy, good rapport, although he knew the thirty-two-year hospital veteran wouldn't hesitate to tell him when she thought he was wrong.

"She fainted," he told her, crossing over to the empty stall.

"Probably not the first time that's happened to you, I'd wager," Jill commented dryly.

On her way to answer a call from another patient, she paused to pull aside the white blanket and sheet on the bed for him. When Georges deposited the unconscious woman on the bed, Jill took off her shoes. After putting them into a plastic bag, the nurse placed it beneath the bed, then pulled the blanket up over the young woman.

"Need anything else?" she asked him. "Other than privacy?"

Sometimes, Georges thought, his reputation kept people from taking him seriously. Usually, it didn't bother him, but he wanted to make sure that the nurse understood this was on the level. "Jill, the woman's been in an accident."

Jill raised her hands to stop him before he could go on. "I know, I know, I saw her grandfather being wheeled out of here to X-ray. Orderly almost popped a wheelie moving by me so fast." Sympathy crinkled along her all-but-unlined face as she looked down at Vienna. And then the next second, she regained her flippant facade. "Well, you know where all the doctor tools are." She patted his back. "Call if you need me." As she began to walk out of the stall, Vienna moaned. Jill paused to wink knowingly at him. "Sounds to me like she's got the sounds down right. You don't want people talking. I'd leave the curtain open if I were you."

Jill left to see about her patient.

Moaning again, Vienna stirred and then opened her eyes. The second after she did, she realized that she was in a horizontal position. She would have bolted upright much too fast, but firm hands on her shoulders pushed her back down onto the mattress.

She blinked and looked up at Georges. Breathing a sigh of relief, she shaded her eyes. "Oh God, what happened?"

"You almost had a close encounter with the hospital floor." Her eyes widened. He found it incredibly appealing. Innocent and vulnerable and somehow sensuous all at the same time. "I caught you just in time."

Well, at least she hadn't made a complete fool of herself, Vienna thought. "That's twice you've come to my rescue."

He did his best to look serious as he nodded.

"Third time and you have to grant me a wish." Again her eyes widened, but this time, he thought he saw a wariness in them. Was she afraid of him? he suddenly wondered. Or had his teasing words triggered a memory she didn't welcome? "I'm kidding," he told her.

"I know that." Digging her knuckles into the mattress on either side of her, Vienna tried to get up for a second time. With the same outcome. He pushed her gently back on the bed. This time, it required a little more force than before.

She was a stubborn one, he thought. "You're not going anywhere until I check you over," he told her.

She began to shake her head, then stopped when tiny little devils with pointy hammers popped up to begin wreaking havoc. Pressing her lips together, willing the pain to go away, she looked up at him. "I'm all right," she insisted.

His eyes swept over her. Georges couldn't help smiling in appreciation. *Now there's an understatement.*

"Be that as it may, I'd like to make sure for myself." Reaching for an instrument to check her pupils, he turned on the light and aimed the pinprick directly at her right eye. "Look up, please."

She resisted, drawing back her head. "This really isn't necessary."

He pointed up to a spot on the ceiling and tried again. "Humor me."

Vienna sighed and stared up at the imaginary spot where he pointed. When he switched eyes and pointed to another area, she complied again.

Georges withdrew the instrument, shutting off the light. "Well?" she asked impatiently.

He returned the instrument to its place. "You don't appear to have a concussion."

"That's because I don't."

"But you did faint," he reminded her. And that could be a symptom of a lot of things—or mean nothing at all. He liked erring on the side of caution when it came to patients. "I could order a set of scans done—"

Vienna cut him off at the pass. "Not on me you can't." She said the words with a smile, but her tone was firm. She knew her own body and there was nothing wrong. Besides, if she was in the hospital as a patient, she might not be able to be with her grandfather and he was all that mattered. "I just got a little frazzled, that's all." Throwing off the covers from her legs, she swung her legs over the side of the bed. As she slid off the bed, she looked down on the floor and her bare feet. There were no shoes in sight. "Now if you could just tell me where my shoes are, I'll be all set."

For a moment, he thought of pleading ignorance,

but he had a feeling that being barefoot would not be enough to keep her here. Bending down, he retrieved the plastic bag from beneath the bed and handed it to her.

"It wouldn't hurt for you to stay overnight for observation, either."

Vienna took out her high heels and, placing them on the floor, stepped into the shoes. It struck Georges that he'd seldom seen anyone move so gracefully.

"Maybe not," she allowed, "but it would be a waste of time and money. I didn't even hit my head."

The hell she didn't. "Then what's this?" Georges asked as he moved back wispy blond bangs from her forehead. A nice-sized bump had begun to form above her right eye. He ran his thumb ever so lightly across it.

Vienna tried not to wince in response, but he saw the slight movement that indicated pain.

She feathered her fingers just on the outer edges of the area and shrugged. "Okay, maybe I did hit my head, but not so that I saw stars," she insisted. "It was my grandfather who got the brunt of the impact." Even as she said it, she could see the events moving in slow motion in her mind's eye. It was a struggle not to shiver. Her expression turned somber. When she spoke, her voice was hushed. Fearful. "How is he?"

"You haven't been out that long," he told her.

"Your grandfather's not back from X-ray yet." Pausing, he studied her for a second.

She shifted slightly, trying to stand as straight as she could. She did *not* want to argue about getting more tests again. "What?"

"Just before you took your unofficial 'nap,'" he said tactfully, "you were about to go to the registration desk to give the administrative assistant your grandfather's insurance information."

Now she remembered, Vienna thought. Edging over to the front of the stall, she inadvertently brushed up against the doctor and instantly felt her body tightening.

Reflexes alive and well, she congratulated herself.

Taking a deep breath, she announced, "Okay, let's go."

But he didn't seem all that ready to take her where she needed to go. Instead, he regarded her for another long moment, as if he expected her to faint again. "You're sure you're up to it?"

In response, she left the curtained enclosure. He quickly fell into step beside her, indicating that she needed to turn right at the end of the hallway. Vienna noticed several nurses watching them as they passed.

"Do you take such good care of all your patients?" she asked.

He appeared to consider her question, then dead-panned, "Only the ones I rescue from a burning car."

"Oh." A smile flickered across her lips, teasing dimples into existence on either cheek. "Lucky thing for me."

They walked through a set of swinging doors. As he brought her over to the first available space in the registration area, his cell phone began to ring.

"She has insurance information about a patient who was just brought in to the E.R.," he told the young girl behind the desk, then turned to Vienna as the phone rang again. "I've got to take this."

Vienna nodded. "Of course."

Taking the cell out of his jacket pocket as he moved away from the desk, Georges glanced down at the number. And winced inwardly.

Diana.

He'd completely forgotten about her. And about his date. He supposed if he hurried, he could still salvage some of the evening.

Georges was considering the option when he saw two policemen entering the E.R., coming from within the hospital rather than via the back entrance the way they had. By their unhurried demeanor, intuition told him the patrolmen were here to see Vienna. Since he'd seen everything that had gone down, that made him a material witness. Which meant that he was going to have to stick around to give his statement, as well.

That made his mind up for him.

Flipping the phone open on the fifth ring, he turned away from the desk. "Diana, hi. I am so sorry. I know I'm late, but I was involved in an accident—"

"An accident?" the voice on the other end repeated breathlessly. "Are you all right?"

"Yes, but the police just got here and I'm going to have to give them my statement. I've got no idea how long this is going to take." He caught himself looking over toward Vienna, wondering if she was going to be up to this. "I'm afraid that I'm going to need a rain check."

"This is Southern California. It doesn't rain here this time of year," Diana reminded him. But she didn't sound angry, just disappointed.

"We can do our own rain dance," he promised, lowering his voice.

He heard her laugh and felt a sense of satisfaction. She'd forgiven him. "That I'd like to see. All right, call me, lover, whenever you're free."

"Count on it," he told her. Ending the call, he flipped the phone closed and pocketed it again. Georges turned around just in time to see the two policemen position themselves on both sides of Vienna's chair. That same protective instinct that had had him throwing his body over hers when the car burst into flames stirred inside his chest.

He quickly crossed back to her, but he was

looking at the patrolmen as he approached. "Can I be of any help, officers?" he asked easily.

The younger of the two policeman gave him a once-over before speaking. "That all depends. You have any information about this car accident on PCH that was reported?"

Boy, have I got some information for you, he thought. Out loud, he said, "As a matter of fact, I do. But first, how did you find out about it?" he asked. He'd given Vienna the number to the hospital to summon an ambulance, not 911.

The younger of the two looked reluctant to divulge any information at all. When he remained silent, his partner said, "Paramedics called it in. Someone named Howard. Told us where to find you." The last statement was directed to Vienna.

Howard. He should have known, Georges thought. The EMT wasn't kidding when he talked about adhering to the rules.

Georges glanced over toward an alcove. E.R. doctors typically retreated there to write their reports without being disturbed. The area was empty at the moment.

"Why don't we move over there, out of the way?" he suggested, indicating the alcove. Not waiting for the policemen to agree, he put his hand beneath Vienna's elbow and helped her up from the chair.

"You a doctor?" the other policeman, older than

his partner by at least a decade, asked as he followed behind them.

Taking out the badge that was still in his pocket, Georges hung it about his neck. "Yes."

"Lucky for the people involved," the older patrolman commented. As the tallest, he stood on the outer perimeter of the space, allowing his partner and the other two to assemble within a space that normally held no more than two.

The patrolmen left half an hour later, satisfied with the report they'd gotten and armed with the make and model, as well as license plate number, of the hit-and-run driver's vehicle. The younger patrolman had even cracked a slight smile. The older one promised they would be in touch the moment there was something to report.

Vienna had held up well during the questioning, Georges thought as the two men in blue took their leave, but now she looked drained. Concern returned.

The moment the policeman walked away from the alcove, Vienna turned toward him and put her hand on his arm, securing his attention. He thought she was going to ask if she could lie down again.

Instead, she asked, "Could you go see how my grandfather's doing?"

"Sure." Glancing to the side, he saw the administrative assistant they'd initially been talking to standing in the corridor, shifting her weight from foot to foot. Rather than ask the woman if anything was wrong, Georges crossed to her and used his body to block her view of Vienna. And vice versa.

"Something wrong?" he asked, his voice low enough not to carry back to the alcove just in case the assistant had come to say something about Vienna's grandfather.

The assistant looked uncomfortable being pushy, but her job demanded it. "I still need that insurance information. All I've got is the guy's name and half an address. I need more."

Relieved that it wasn't anything more serious, Georges nodded sympathetically. "Sure you do." But in his opinion, Vienna needed a break. She'd been answering questions steadily for twenty minutes. He'd given his statement to the older of the policemen while she had been grilled by the younger one. "Look, how about I get the insurance information to you in a little while?"

The assistant hesitated, wavering. "Technically, you're not supposed to start any work on him until I have *something* for his record."

"You have something," he told her smoothly, placing his hand on hers and turning her away from the alcove and back toward her own area. "You have my word." Covertly, he read the name on her tag and added, "Amanda."

The personal touch, he'd found time and again, always helped to move things along in the right direction.

Amanda seemed flustered now, as well as uncertain. "You sure you'll get that information to me?"

Georges nodded. "Just as soon as I can, Amanda," he promised, then winked as if that made it their little secret.

Amanda was already backing away to return to her desk. "I guess it's okay."

He flashed a grin. "You're a doll." The blush that rose to the woman's cheeks told him that he had sealed the bargain.

Going back into the rear of the E.R., it didn't take him long to find Murphy. The latter was dealing with a screaming infant with colic. The first-time parents both seemed at the end of their collective emotional ropes. Flanking both sides of the raised railings of the baby's bed, they peppered Murphy with questions, one dovetailing into another.

When he approached Murphy, the physician looked relieved to see him.

"Excuse me for a moment," he said, extricating himself from the circle of noise. Moving toward the side, Murphy shook his head. "I'm going to have to have my hearing checked after tonight. I think I've lost the ability to hear anything at a high frequency."

Blowing out a breath, he glanced up at Georges. "You're going to ask me about the old man, right?"

Georges saw no point in wasting time, even though he knew Murphy wasn't anxious to get back to his tiny patient and his overwrought parents. "Are his films back yet?"

Murphy nodded. "Just. I've put out a call for an internal surgeon and I want a consult with Dr. Greywolf," he added, mentioning one of Blair's top heart surgeons.

"What's wrong with him?" Georges pressed.

Murphy rattled off the important particulars. "His spleen's been damaged, his liver was bruised in the accident and several ribs were cracked, not to mention that he did have a minor heart attack. Nice work bringing him around, by the way."

It never hurt to have one of the chief attendings compliment your work, Georges thought. "Thanks." But right now, he was more interested in the answer to his next question. "Who'd you call for the surgery?"

"Rob Schulman. He's on call for the night. I'm trying to get Darren Patterson to act as assistant on the procedures, but so far, Patterson's not answering his page."

Georges didn't even have to think about it. "I can assist," he volunteered. Murphy eyed him skeptically. All surgical residents were eager to operate whenever possible, but this went beyond wanting to put in time in the O.R. He felt an obligation to the old man to see things through. "I've assisted Schulman before. If Patterson doesn't answer by the time Schulman gets here—"

"You scrub in," Murphy concluded, agreeing. The night shift was always down on viable personnel, and they worked with what they could get on short notice.

The baby's screams grew louder again. Murphy gritted his teeth. "Any chance you want to fill in for me until Schulman shows up?"

Georges laughed and shook his head. "Not a chance. I put in my eighteen hours today."

"Then why aren't you dead on your feet?"

Georges grinned as he spread his hands innocently. "Clean living."

"Not from what I hear," Murphy responded. He turned around to walk back to the shrieking baby's stall. "Into the Valley of Death rode the six hundred," he muttered under his breath.

"A doctor who quotes Tennyson. That should look good on your résumé," Georges commented.

Murphy said something unintelligible as he disappeared into the stall.

Georges made his way back to Vienna.

The second she saw him, she was on her feet, her eyes opened wide like Bambi.

"My grandfather…"

Her voice trailed off. She couldn't bring herself

to complete the question, afraid of being too optimistic. Afraid of the alternative even more. She held her breath, waiting for Georges to answer her.

"Is going to need surgery," he told her, saying only what they both already knew. "He got a little banged up inside and we're going to fix that," he assured Vienna in a calm, soothing voice.

Relief wafted over her. Her grandfather was still alive. There was hope. And then she replayed the doctor's words in her head.

"We?" she questioned. "Then you'll be the one operating on him?"

"Dr. Schulman will be performing the surgery. He's one of the best in the country. I'll be assisting him if they can't find anyone else."

She took hold of his hand, her eyes on his, riveting him in place. "I don't want anyone else," she told him with such feeling it all but took his breath away. "I want you. I want you to be there."

"They're trying to locate another surgeon to assist, but—"

"No," she interrupted. "You. I want you." Her fingers closed over his hand. "You'll help. I can feel it. It's important that you be there for him during the operation. Please."

Georges heard himself saying, "All right," but, like a ventriloquist, she was the one who was drawing the words from his lips.

Chapter Four

The next moment, Vienna suddenly pulled back.

Georges probably thought she was crazy, she thought, and she didn't want to alienate him. But she was certain that he *had* to be in the operating room.

It wasn't that she thought of herself as clairvoyant, she just had these…*feelings,* for lack of a better word. Feelings that came to her every so often.

Feelings that always turned out to be true.

She'd had one of those feelings the day her parents were killed.

Vienna had been only eight at the time, still very much a child, but somehow, as they bid her goodbye, saying they would see her that evening, she instinctively knew that she was seeing Bill and Theresa Hollenbeck for the last time. She'd clung to each of her parents in turn, unwilling to release them, unable to make them understand that if they walked out that door, if they drove to Palm Springs to meet with her mother's best friend and that woman's fiancé, that they would never see another sunrise.

God knew she'd tried to tell them, but they had laughed and hugged her, and told her not to worry. That she was just held captive by an overactive imagination. And her grandfather's stories. Amos Schwarzwalden, her mother's father, was visiting from Austria at the time and they left her with him.

And drove out of her life forever.

The accident happened at six-thirty that evening. It was a huge pileup on I-5 that made all the local papers and the evening news. Seven cars had plowed into one another after a drunk driver had lost control of his car. A semi had swerved to avoid hitting the careening vehicle—and wound up hitting the seven other cars instead.

Miraculously, there'd only been two casualties. Tragically, those two casualties had been her parents.

It was the first time Vienna could remember ever having one of those "feelings."

After that, there were other times, other occasions where a sense of uneasiness warned her that something bad was going to happen. But the feeling never came at regular intervals or even often. It didn't occur often enough for her grandfather, who was the only one she shared this feeling with, to think she had some sort of extraordinary power. She didn't consider herself a seer or someone with "the sight" as those in the old country were wont to say.

But her "intuitions" occurred just often enough for her not to ignore them when they did happen. And even though they had not warned her of the car accident that had nearly stolen her grandfather from her, they now made her feel that if this man who had come to their rescue was not in the O.R. when her grandfather was being operated on, something very serious was going to happen. Something that would not allow her grandfather to be part of her life anymore.

Her eyes met Georges' and she flashed a rueful smile that instantly took him captive.

"I'm sorry, I didn't mean to sound as if I was coming unhinged," Vienna apologized, but all the same, she continued holding on to his arm. "But I really do feel very strongly about this," she emphasized. "You *have* to be in the operating room with my grandfather."

Georges could all but feel the urgency rippling through her, transmitting itself to him. The woman was dead serious. They were running out of time and as far as he knew, Patterson had still not been located.

"All right," Georges agreed gently. "I'll go talk to the surgeon." Placing his hand over hers, he squeezed it lightly and gave her an encouraging smile. "You sit tight, all right?"

Vienna was barely aware of nodding her head. She forced a smile to her lips.

"All right," she murmured. "And thank you. Again."

He merely nodded and then hurried away.

In the locker room, he quickly changed into scrubs. As he closed the locker door, he felt as if he was getting a second wind. Or was that his third one? He wasn't altogether sure. By all rights, at this point in his day—or night—he should have been dead on his feet, looking forward to nothing more than spending the rest of the night in a reclining position—as he'd planned with Diana.

Instead, as he headed to scrub in, he felt suddenly invigorated. Ready to leap tall buildings in a single bound. The prospect of facing a surgery always did that to him. It put him on his toes and, Georges found, instantly transformed him into the very best version of himself.

He all but burst into the area where the sinks were and after greeting the surgeon, began the laborious process of getting ready to perform the procedure—in double time.

Rob Schulman was carefully scrubbing the area between his fingers with a small scrub brush. Every surgeon had superstitions. Schulman's was to use a new scrub brush for every surgery. He glanced over toward Georges.

He seemed mildly amused at the energy he witnessed in the other man.

"Someday, Georges, you're going to have to tell me what kind of vitamins you're on." When Georges looked over toward him quizzically, he elaborated. "I saw you eight hours ago and they tell me that except for two hours, you've been here all this time. What kind of a deal with the devil did you make?" Schulman asked. He paused to rotate his neck. Several cracks were heard to echo through the small area. The surgical nurses, waiting their turn, exchanged smiles. "Why is it you're not falling on your face?"

"I scheduled that for after the surgery," Georges replied with an easy air that hid the electrical current all but racing through him. Done, he gave his hands another once-over, just in case. "I want to thank you for letting me scrub in."

Schulman laughed softly to himself, the high-pitched sound incongruous with man's considerable bulk. "You're welcome, but this time, it's more of a matter of supply and demand, Georges. Murphy told me that they can't find another assistant in time."

They could have opted to wait. Or, in an emergency, Murphy could have scrubbed in. Carefree to a fault, Georges still knew better than to take anything for granted. He inclined his head toward the senior internal surgeon. "I'll take what I can get."

Schulman concentrated on his nail beds, scrubbing hard. "They tell me you brought him in." He raised his brown eyes toward Georges for a second. "Hunting down your own patients these days?"

Georges pretended he hadn't heard that line twice already this evening and flashed an easy smile at the man.

"I was on Pacific Coast Highway," he told Schulman. "The accident happened right behind me."

"Lucky for the driver you were there," Schulman commented. Finished, he leaned his elbow against the metal faucet handles and turned off the water. Bracing himself, he looked toward the swinging double doors that led into the operating room. "All right, let's see if I can keep that luck going."

Georges nodded. Finished with his own preparations for the surgery, he followed Schulman into the O.R., his own hands raised and ready to have surgical gloves slipped over them.

An eerie feeling passed over him the moment he'd said the words. Exactly one moment after he had pointed out to Schulman that an artery the latter had cauterized wasn't, in fact, completely sealed.

With the old man's organs all vying for space, it had been an easy matter to miss the slow seepage. The surgeon was focused on what he was doing, removing the spleen and resectioning the liver by removing a small, damaged portion no more than the size of a quarter. As all this went on—not to mention the presence of various instruments, suction tubes and clamps within the small area—the tiny bit of oozing had almost been overlooked. *Would* have been overlooked had something not caught his eye in that region.

He still wasn't sure exactly what had prompted him to push back the retractor and look, but he was so glad he had. The seepage could have cost the patient his life.

I don't want anyone else. I want you. I want you to be there. It's important that you be there for him during the operation.

Had she known? Had the blonde with the intensely blue eyes somehow known that this was why he had to be inside the O.R.?

Lily believed in things that went beyond religion and beyond any reason known to man. Ever since he could remember, she made it a point to rule out nothing. Not spirits, not things beyond the realm of the everyday and the norm. Periodically, his mother would seek the guidance of a palm reader and have her future told.

According to his mother, that was how she'd known which of the men in her life to marry and which merely to enjoy. In the end, her insecurity and restlessness had her leaving all of them, husband or lover, but she claimed that her fortune-teller helped her "see" which path to take.

Both Philippe and Alain placed no stock in that, pooh-poohing her fondness for fortune-tellers as just another eccentric attribute that contributed to her being Lily Moreau. But he was inclined to go along with the that line from *Hamlet*. That there were more things in heaven and on earth than could possibly be dreamt of in anyone's philosophy.

Now, as he watched Schulman swiftly reassess the situation, he caught himself wondering about the blonde he'd left in the surgical lounge.

Was the woman clairvoyant?

He didn't know. Didn't know if he actually believed in clairvoyance—but she *had* been adamant that he be here in the O.R. And if he *hadn't* been here, her grandfather would presently be bleeding out. By the time Amos's condition worsened enough for them to reopen him again and locate the bleeding artery, it might have very well been too late to remedy the situation.

"Nice catch, Georges," Schulman was saying as he

called for more sponges to help clean out the blood from the small cavity. Unlike some physicians, the internal surgeon had no problem with giving credit where he felt credit was due. "You very well might have saved this man's life." Schulman glanced up and his eyes above the mask were smiling as they looked at Georges. "Again. When this is over, the man should adopt you. Or at least put you in his will."

Georges made no comment. He was still trying to sort things out in his head.

It was another three hours before the surgery was finally over.

Feeling drained and spent and yet experiencing that exhilarating high that always accompanied any surgery he was part of, Georges untied his mask. For the moment, he left it dangling around his neck as he walked back to the sinks just beyond the operating room. Behind him, Amos Schwarzwalden was being wheeled through the opposite set of doors into the recovery room where he would remain for the next hour or so to be observed.

As always, washing up after a surgery took far less time than presurgical preparation. Finished, Georges dried his hands and happened to glance down at his scrubs. He realized that if he was going to see Vienna, he needed to stop off at his locker and change. His shirt had her grandfather's blood on it.

Not exactly the best way to look when he went to give her a firsthand report about the way the surgery had gone.

"Any more people you want me to operate on?" Schulman asked as he finished up himself.

"No, not tonight," Georges answered.

"Good." He glanced around the area. "Then I bid you all good night, people."

The last thing Schulman did before he left was throw away the scrub brush he'd used on his nails.

Georges hurried to the locker room for a clean shirt, not wanting to keep Vienna anxiously waiting any longer than she had to.

Vienna was the only person waiting in the surgical lounge.

Ordinarily, during the course of a normal day, the large, spacious room, with its soft lighting, comfortable sofas and large selection of surprisingly up-to-date reading material, was anywhere from half to completely full with anxious friends and relatives waiting to hear the outcome of their loved one's surgery. But at this hour of the night, the area was usually empty.

Not tonight.

Vienna had the considerable length of the room to move around in. Initially, she'd sat, first on one sofa, then another, then yet another, until she had, like Goldilocks, tried out every seat in the lounge. She'd also looked through every piece of literature in the lounge. Or attempted to.

The pages had moved, and so had her eyes, as she flipped from magazine to magazine. Not a single word had stuck during the course of her entire waiting period. So she had given up and wound up pacing from side to side, trying desperately to plumb the depth of her optimism and make herself truly believe that everything was going to be all right, just as the doctor had said.

Just as he'd promised.

But try as she may, and despite the fact that he had gone in as she'd asked him to, she still could not allow herself to fully relax. Worry became her constant companion.

Her face, a battlefield between concern and her inherent optimism, which ordinarily insisted on seeing the best in any situation, lit up the moment she saw Georges approaching in the distance. She didn't wait for him to come to her. Instead, she rushed over to him before Georges had a chance to reach the lounge.

Holding her breath, Vienna searched his face for a sign that she'd been right to beg him to go into the O.R. That the doctor fate had brought into her life so unexpectedly had saved her grandfather.

"Well?" she cried, her voice all but cracking.

He smiled at her. "Your grandfather's going to be fine," he told her.

It amazed him that yet again, a fresh wave of energy, coming out of nowhere, seemed to find him. Three was usually his limit for one twenty-four-hour period, not four.

The next moment, her face glowing with relief, Vienna threw her arms around his neck. But instead of kissing him the way she had the first time, she turned her face into his chest and began to sob.

"Hey, it's okay," Georges told her soothingly. After a beat, he closed his arms around her and slowly rubbed her back, the way he would a distraught child. "There's no reason to cry. Your grandfather came through it like a trouper." Despite the fact that Lily Moreau was the personification of drama, Georges always felt at a loss when faced with a woman's tears. Especially when those tears had nothing to do with sorrow. Why would a woman cry when she was happy? "We fixed everything that was wrong with him."

Georges held her for as long as she seemed to need it, secretly enjoying the warmth of her body against his, murmuring words of comfort. But when she finally stepped back, wiping away the tears from her cheeks and pulling herself together, he couldn't hold his question back any longer.

"How did you know?" he asked her.

Blinking back the last of her tears from her lashes, Vienna lifted her head. Though her eyes weren't swollen, her cheeks were streaked with tears. Georges reached into his pocket and found a handkerchief. Handing it to Vienna, he drew back just far enough to study her face.

"How did you know?" he asked again.

"Know what?"

Vienna let out a long, ragged breath, then drew in another one, trying to steady herself. Trying to sound normal again. For more than an hour, despite all her best efforts, she had begun to succumb to fear. She loved the old man who had dedicated his life to her, who had given up his home, his business in Austria, to come to America and be her family. Steadier now, she wiped her cheeks and looked at Georges, waiting.

"How did you know about the nicked artery?"

Vienna shook her head, silently indicating that she didn't really know what he was referring to.

"You said I needed to be there."

Now she understood. And wondered if he did.

Her eyes held his for a moment before she said anything. "And did you?"

He thought she was referring to his being in the O.R. in general. "Well, yes. The surgeon, Dr. Schulman, needed an assistant for the procedures." But she already knew that, he thought. Was there something he was missing? "But I'm talking about the fact that if I hadn't been there, Dr. Schulman would have missed the nicked artery. He'd cauterized it, but for some reason, and this is pretty rare—" he underscored that since Schulman was top in his field "—it didn't take. There was still a tiny pinprick opened and it was oozing blood. It was just enough to turn your grand-father septic if it hadn't been detected."

She nodded her head as if reviewing something that she already knew. "And you detected it."

It wasn't a question.

After a moment, Georges nodded. "Yes, I did." His eyes narrowed as he took back the handkerchief she held out to him. "You knew I would," he realized out loud. "How did you know?"

Looking away, Vienna shrugged, trying to push the question, the situation, away, as well. Without success. She knew she owed the surgeon before her more than that. He'd listened to her, come through for her. Because of him, Amos Schwarzwalden, the only living member of her family, was still alive. She owed this man more than she could ever begin to repay.

But he probably wasn't going to believe her, she thought.

Looking back at him, she shrugged again. "I don't know how I knew. I just did." Vienna moist-ened her lips, then indicated that he should follow her to the closest sofa. She wanted some sort of shelter, for herself and for what she was about to say.

When he sat down beside her, she continued.

"Sometimes," she confided, leaning her body into his and lowering her voice, "I get these…feelings." She raised her eyes to his face, waiting for him to laugh. When he didn't, she experienced a tremendous wave of relief. He believed her. Or, at least, he didn't disbelieve her.

Not yet.

She was serious, he thought. "What kind of 'feelings'?" Georges wanted to know.

She didn't know how better to describe it than that. "Just feelings. Premonitions," she added in hopes that the word might make it clearer for him. "Like I know something is going to happen. I don't know why I know," she added before he could ask. "And it doesn't happen very often, maybe a handful of times since I was a little girl. But when it does, I'm usually right."

It was a lie, but, in her opinion, a necessary one. She had no way of knowing how he might take the information that when these feelings came upon her, she wasn't "usually" right; she was *always* right. For the time being, she sensed that maybe this would be just a wee bit too spooky a revelation to share with the good doctor.

Even now, he seemed to be watching her a little

uncertainly. Not that she could blame him. If their positions were switched, she'd probably feel the same way.

In the end, none of that mattered. Her grandfather was going to be all right. Because Georges Armand had been in the right place at the right time. Twice.

Chapter Five

Vienna looked tired, Georges thought. Now that her grandfather's surgery was over, there was no immediate reason for her to stay.

"Why don't I take you home?" Georges suggested. "Your home," he added in case she thought he was suggesting something.

Georges was aware of the way his offer might be misconstrued because somewhere in the recesses of his mind, the thought about taking this woman home, *his* home, had occurred to him. Since she wasn't a patient of his, there was no conflict of interest—only interest, a great deal of interest—

now that the operation was behind him and he could allow himself to really look at her.

He liked what he saw. A delicate, slender blonde who didn't fold at the first sign of adversity. It was a good trait to have. Being exceedingly attractive wasn't exactly a minus, either.

But Vienna shook her head in response to his offer. "No, that's all right. I'll just stay here and wait to see my grandfather."

Maybe she didn't realize how long it would be before the old man would be moved to his room. "Most likely, your grandfather's going to be in recovery for a couple of hours."

The news didn't seem to daunt Vienna. She sounded almost cheerful as she replied, "I can wait."

"And even after they move him, he probably won't be very lucid. Most likely, he'll just sleep."

She knew the doctor meant well, but he just didn't understand. The very fact that the old man was alive heartened her. "I can watch him breathe."

Georges studied her for a long moment. "He means a great deal to you, doesn't he?"

Vienna smiled to herself, thinking how very inadequate that phrase was when it came to expressing how she felt about Amos Schwarzwalden. "You have no idea."

Well, if she was going to stay, he didn't want

her being by herself. "Is there anyone I can call to stay with you?"

Vienna didn't even pause to think. She shook her head. "We're relatively new here in Southern California. We've only been in Bedford a little over six months."

The late hour had done nothing to abate his curiosity about her. Was there a husband in the wings? A significant other she didn't want disturbed?

"By 'we'…" He allowed his voice to trail off, waiting for her to fill in the blank.

She smiled at his fishing. "I mean my grandfather and me."

It wasn't the most common combination when it came to family members. He heard himself asking, "Where are your parents?"

He saw a little of the color leave Vienna's face and knew he'd stumbled onto ground he had no business crossing.

"Both gone," she told him, doing her best to sound matter-of-fact. She didn't quite pull it off. "They died in a car crash when I was eight. My grandfather was visiting from Austria at the time and staying with us." She tried not to think as she spoke. Even after all these years, it still hurt. "When the accident happened, he sold his business in Vienna and stayed in America with me." She looked up at him, wanting Georges to understand why the man meant so very much to her. Why she would do anything for him. "He turned his whole world upside down for me because he didn't want to take me away from the home where I'd always lived."

Selflessness was a rare thing. The closest he'd come to it in his own life was Philippe. His mother, bless her, went by a whole other set of rules. It didn't make her a bad mother, just different. "Sounds like your grandfather is a hell of a man."

"He is that." Leaning toward him, Vienna placed her hand on top of his. But it was her eyes that seemed to touch him, her eyes that said more than her words could. "Thank you for saving him."

He'd never had a problem accepting gratitude. To him, it was all part of the field he was in. But he couldn't remember ever seeing it look or sound so eloquent and yet so simple.

"You've already thanked me," he reminded her.

Vienna slowly moved her head from side to side. "Never enough." And then she grinned as she withdrew her hand from his. "You're entitled to free baked goods for life."

He could have sworn that he still felt her fingers against his skin. "Excuse me?"

"We moved to Southern California for his health," she told him, "but my grandfather isn't the kind of man who can stand doing nothing. So he opened a bakery in Newport Beach. He was a pastry chef in his native country," she said proudly. "In this country, too. When he came to New York to raise me, he opened up a small bakery off Fifth Avenue. After a while, so many people started coming, he had to buy out the store next to him and expand." By the time he sold his bakery, it was a tremendous cash cow. "I'm sure that once he's back on his feet, my grandfather's going to insist that you come by—on a regular basis, most likely."

Georges rolled the idea over in his head. He had to admit, this did open up possibilities. He wouldn't mind seeing the blonde again after her grandfather checked out of the hospital.

"You work with him?" he asked.

She nodded. "I run the business end of it for him." And had since she graduated with a business degree from Columbia University. "But he's taught me a little about baking. I can't hold a candle to him—his pastries have to be tied down to keep them from floating away off the plate—but you won't have to run to the medicine cabinet for mouthwash after eating one of mine."

Not if her pastries were anything like her kisses, Georges caught himself thinking. "Well, I'll have to come by, then." And then he realized he was missing one crucial piece of information. "What's the shop called?"

"Vienna's Finest." When he looked at her, amused,

she blushed. He found the added shade on her cheeks intriguing. "Grandfather was born in Vienna and it was his favorite city when he was a boy. My mother was born there, too," she added. "She and my father met when he was in the army stationed near there."

"How did you come to be named after the city?" he asked.

"My mother said she wanted to do something to make her feel closer to her father, so she named me after his favorite place. You have to admit, it's better than calling me Amos," she added with a fond smile.

There was a sadness in her eyes, Georges noticed. A sadness he found himself drawn to even though, at the same time, he wanted to erase it from her soul.

He changed the subject. "So there's no one I can call for you?"

Vienna shook her head. "Grandfather knows a lot of people and they're all very fond of him, but there's no one to rouse out of bed at one in the morning."

Even if there was, she wouldn't have allowed it. She couldn't think of anything worse than getting a call in the middle of the night, saying someone had been hurt and was in the hospital. The call about her parents' accident had come in the middle of the night. It had taken that long to identify them. To this day, she cringed whenever the phone rang after she went to bed.

"I'll be fine," she assured him with feeling. "I'll just curl up here—" she nodded toward the sofa "—and wait until they take him to his room."

"Well, then I guess you'll want some coffee." He stopped in his tracks and turned around to give her another choice. "Or some chicken soup. They have some in the vending machine by the nurses' station on the second floor. I can bring you back a container. It's surprisingly not bad."

She noticed that he didn't say *good* and laughed. "Not exactly a ringing endorsement," she observed. "Doctor's orders?"

"Yeah, maybe." If that's what it took to get her to eat or drink something. As he recalled, she'd had neither since she'd gotten to the hospital. "If you're going to play Florence Nightingale, you're going to need to keep your strength up."

She supposed that made sense. Vienna nodded, making her choice. "Chicken soup, then. But I can get it. You need to go home, or wherever it was that you were going before we all but crashed into you and pulled you into our lives."

"It's too late for 'wherever.'" If he were being honest with himself, he no longer had a desire to see Diana tonight. He'd gotten too wrapped up in the surgery to wind down enough for the kind of evening he shared with her. "And I can always go home. Besides—" he glanced at his watch, a Rolex that was a gift from his late father "—at this point, I'm closer to my next shift than not."

Vienna frowned. The man should have been asleep hours ago. "Now you're making me feel bad." At least, for him. But then, if he hadn't been there, her grandfather might not be in the recovery room right now.

"No reason." He hadn't said what he had to make her feel guilty; it had just been a fact, duly noted. "Didn't you know? Doctors run on batteries the first ten years of their careers." He began to walk toward the back elevators. "I'll be right back," he promised.

She nodded, settling back against the cushions. She tried not to sigh. "I'll be right here."

When he returned fifteen minutes later, true to her word, Vienna was exactly where he'd left her: sitting on the sofa closest to the entrance.

But her eyes were shut and she appeared to be dozing. Very quietly, Georges placed the container of chicken soup on the circular table in front of the sofa and within her easy reach once she woke up. Straightening, he wondered if he could borrow a blanket from the emergency room in order to cover her. Without the warm press of interacting bodies, the hospital felt cold.

As he began to tiptoe away, heading toward the E.R., he heard her say, "There's no reason to tread so softly. I'm not asleep."

Georges turned back around to face her. "You're eyes were shut."

She stifled a yawn, pressing her lips together until it faded. "I was just resting them. I might not be a doctor, but I don't need much sleep, either. Especially when my nerves are all in knots."

She'd taken off her shoes and had tucked her feet under her on the sofa. She stretched out now, swinging them down. Her bare feet brushed against the indoor-outdoor carpeting as she reached for the container he'd brought back for her. Vienna pressed a perforated square on the plastic lid and slowly took a sip.

"Mmm, good," she commented. Savoring her first taste, she smiled fondly. "Grandfather always says there is nothing like chicken soup to make you feel better." She paused, as if debating telling him the next part. "I drank a lot of chicken soup that first year after my parents died," she added softly.

She raised her eyes to his as she cradled the container between her hands. There was sympathy in his eyes. Or was that pity? Sympathy was all right, but she didn't want pity. That was what she got for opening up like that, Vienna silently upbraided herself.

"No word yet, right?" She punctuated her question by nodding in the general direction of the O.R.

"No," he confirmed. "And no news actually *is* good news in this case. We want your grandfather's progress to be unremarkable—and steady."

She'd drink to that, she thought.

Vienna raised her container slightly, like someone giving a toast. "To unremarkable and steady." For a second, Vienna's eyes shifted over toward him. "And to the remarkable and steady doctor who came to Grandfather's rescue."

Georges shifted to her sofa and took a seat beside her. At this proximity, the bump on her forehead was visible enough for him to examine again.

"Sure I can't talk you into getting a scan of that?" Very lightly, he touched her forehead so she knew what he was referring to. "On me," he added in case she had no medical coverage available.

"A CT scan, the gift for the girl who has everything," Vienna quipped, just before taking another sip of her soup. And then she laughed even as she shook her head. "Not necessary, Doctor. Even my headache's gone." Or almost gone, she amended silently.

He looked dubious. "That could just be shock, masking it."

"Or it could be nothing," she countered. She didn't want him fussing over her. If anything, she wanted him fussing over her grandfather. "I'm very resilient, Doctor."

And then, out of the blue, she thought of her heart and the way she'd had to put all the pieces together after Edward had walked out of her life. Two years gone in a puff of smoke, just like that, without so much as a backward glance. All because he couldn't allow anyone else into the narrow world he'd defined for them, not even her grandfather. Not even after he knew how much the man meant to her. She'd misspent those two years. But it didn't help her heal any faster.

"I've had to be," she added softly, saying the words more to herself than to him.

He looked at her for a long moment, curbing the desire to lose his fingers in her hair. "That sounds like it has a story behind it."

She raised her eyes to his and tried to smile as she banished the memory away. "It does."

"But you're not going to share it," Georges guessed after a beat.

"Not tonight." And then she smiled, adding, "Not until I know you better."

The words echoed within the all but empty room.

They had *future* stamped all over them. It surprised him to realize that he rather savored the unspoken implication. Ordinarily, when someone made any sort of definite plans that involved him and went beyond the weekend or, in rare instances, the following week, alarms would go off in his head, ringing loudly and urging him to end it because he had to move on.

Time to get out of Dodge and head for the next sunrise.

But there were no alarms, no warning bells. Instead, he found himself wondering about the woman beside him. Wondering and wanting to know things about her. Wanting to fill in the myriad of blanks dancing in front of him.

This, too, shall pass, he promised himself. It was just something different, that's all. *She* was something different, he amended. And different had always intrigued him.

"Something to look forward to," he said to her. It earned him another smile. One that seemed to burrow right smack into the middle of his chest.

In a little while, after the soup had been finished and the coffee grown cold, he went to check on Amos's progress.

The sleepy-eyed night nurse informed him that his patient had responded so well to the surgical procedure, the attending physician had decided to move him out of recovery a full half hour before Amos was scheduled to leave.

Georges returned to share his findings with Vienna.

The moment he did, she was on her feet, heading toward the recovery room's outer doors. They arrived just as Amos was about to be transported.

Vienna felt tears gathering in her eyes as she looked down at her grandfather. She didn't bother wiping them away.

Clutching the heavy-duty plastic bag that contained her grandfather's clothes, Vienna walked beside the gurney as the orderly wheeled the sleeping man to the back of the hospital and the service elevators. Georges accompanied them to the third floor, which, for the most part, was designated as the surgical wing.

Every second light was turned off, giving the area almost an eerie atmosphere as, once off the service elevator, they made their way down the corridor.

Amos was placed in a single care unit that was only marginally larger than his space in the recovery room had been. Still, with the right finagling, some space could be found.

"I can have a cot brought in," Georges offered, looking at Vienna, "so you can stretch out a little."

Vienna placed the plastic bag with her grandfather's things into the closet and shut the single door. Her slender shoulders rose and fell in a shrug to Georges' offer. "Stretching out is highly overrated." She nodded at the padded beige chair by the window. "I'll be fine in this chair."

It seemed pointless for her to spend the night in the chair, even though he knew that the heart was not subject to logic. "He's probably not going to wake up between now and morning."

She knew that. Knew that it was better for her grandfather to sleep through what was left of the night. "I don't need him to wake up, Doctor. I just need him to be."

Georges sighed, shaking his head. "Are all Austrians this stubborn?"

Her mouth curved. For the first time, he saw a smile enter her eyes, as well. It took him a second to extricate himself.

"I'm Austrian and one quarter Italian," she informed him. "But yes, to answer your question, they are. And so are Italians."

Georges took the information in stride, nodding. "Then I guess that I haven't got a prayer of talking you out of this."

"'Fraid not."

Vienna moved closer to the bed. Standing over her grandfather for a moment, she brushed back a few gray strands that would have been in his eyes had they been open. Her grandfather had a full head of gray hair, still thick and rich. It was one of the things he was proud of. That and the fact that, at seventy-four, he was still pretty much as strong as an ox, albeit a more mature ox, she'd often teased him.

Be that ox now, Grandfather. Come back to me.

And then she turned to look at Georges. "I will, however, let you get that extra blanket for me if you like."

Georges watched her for a long moment. He'd thought about getting the blanket when she'd been in the surgical lounge, but— "I never said that out loud," he told her slowly. "Are you going to tell me that you read minds, too?"

Her smile was like quicksilver. "I'm not going to say anything of the kind."

Was that because she didn't want to spook him, or because she didn't think she could? It struck him that this whole night was a little on the surreal side. "Then how…"

Vienna casually lifted her shoulders and let them fall again. "Elementary, my dear Watson. You look like the type who likes to take care of people. Covering a sleeping person with a blanket just seems to make sense," she explained.

It was plausible, of course, but he couldn't shake the feeling that he had just stumbled into something that was different. Something he couldn't explain away all that easily.

In addition, he thought as he walked out of the room, in search of said blanket, the way that Vienna seemed to intuit things about him made him feel a little uneasy. Uncertain. He took care of people because he was a doctor, but she made it sound as if what she sensed about him went deeper than that. As if it had roots in something more.

She seemed to know him better than he knew himself.

The next moment, he dismissed the thought, bunching it under the simple truth that he was tired and nothing more.

It seemed like a reasonable enough explanation.

Chapter Six

Ultimately, Vienna dozed for perhaps thirty minutes. Perhaps less.

Restlessness roused her and she wound up shrugging off the blanket and just sitting in the chair, watching her grandfather sleep. And talking to the man who insisted on keeping her company.

Just before dawn, Georges was finally able to convince her to go home. Not to get some well-deserved rest, which would have made sense, but to make sure Vienna's Finest opened on time. It was the only thing that finally got her to consider leaving her grandfather's side.

Her grandfather, Georges pointed out, wouldn't want the customers who came in for their early morning pick-me-up to be disappointed and go away empty-handed. He managed to appeal to her sense of loyalty and to what he surmised was her equally, very deep-seated sense of responsibility.

The idea came to Georges as he heard her make a call on the phone beside Amos's bed at around 3:00 a.m. The call was to someone named Raul who apparently was the baker and made the different confections. From what Georges could piece together, Raul had moved here from New York after they had relocated because he was unwilling to work for anyone else besides Amos.

Raul seemed highly excitable. His voice became very audible on the other end of the line when Vienna told him that she and her grandfather had been in a car accident.

"He's all right, Raul," Vienna assured him quickly, repeating the words several times and striving to sound soothing despite her weariness. "There was a doctor on the scene and he brought us to the hospital."

"On the scene?" Georges heard the man's heavily accented voice fairly shout over the line. "What do you mean, on the scene? Was this doctor the one who caused the accident?"

Vienna glanced over toward Georges and smiled. "No, he was the one who saved my grandfather's life. I just need you to open up the bakery this morning. Can you do that, Raul?"

There was a long pause before Raul answered. When he did, he sounded highly skeptical. "I don't know. Customers…" His voice trailed off for a moment. "I bake, I don't sell."

There was no way to avoid hearing. Georges tapped her on the shoulder. When she looked at him, he suggested, "Why don't you go in and open up the bakery, get things started?"

She thought for a moment. It had been a long time since she'd been behind the counter, not since she'd graduated college. But she supposed it was like swimming. You never quite forgot what to do with your hands. She finally nodded. "I can keep it going until Zelda comes in."

"Zelda?" he asked.

"A part-timer. She comes in around nine to help behind the counter." Vienna turned her attention back to the receiver. Raul could be heard calling to her, asking if she was still there. "Yes, I'm still here, Raul. Business as usual. Just go in and do what you'd do on any other day. I'll be there by six-thirty to handle the rest."

Which was how Georges got her to finally leave the hospital.

* * *

It was just as her newfound knight in shining Armani was turning into the driveway of her house that it suddenly hit her.

Covering her mouth with both hands she uttered a stifled, "Oh God."

Georges nearly swerved, thinking he'd hit something or was about to, most likely some meandering neighborhood pet too low to the ground to see easily. But the driveway stretched out before him debris-free, with not so much as an overzealous grasshopper to squash.

"What?" he demanded a little more sharply than he'd meant to.

She sank back against the back cushion, figuratively and literaly flattened by the weight of her sudden epiphany. "My purse was in the car."

Which was now toast, Georges thought. By the time the fire department had arrived on the scene, on the heels of the ambulance from Blair Memorial, the flames around the car were retreating, leaving a burnt shell in its wake. He'd been so intent on getting her and her grandfather out, he hadn't even thought of anything so trivial as a purse.

Maybe he should have, he thought now. "What was in it?"

She looked devastated, he noted, as she gave him an answer that was universal to women everywhere except for the darkest recesses of the African and South American jungles.

"Everything." With a gut-wrenching sigh, Vienna closed her eyes, momentarily feeling overwhelmed by this latest development. "My wallet, my driver's license, my cell phone, my car keys." Opening her eyes again, she looked at the house and then turned to him. "My house keys."

Parking, Georges pulled up the hand brake and turned the engine off. "You don't keep a spare near the front door?"

The very idea was completely foreign to her. "I'm from New York. We double lock everything. We don't keep keys hidden under a planter so that someone can break in." Still sitting in the car, she looked at the door again. "Oh God, what am I going to do?"

He was thoughtful for a moment. "I think you already covered it."

When she glanced back at him again, she could have sworn that she saw the curve of a smile on his lips. "What?"

"Break in," he replied simply.

She thought of her neighbors. This was a very quiet neighborhood.

"You mean like break a window?" At the first sound of breaking glass, especially at this time of the morning, she had no doubt someone would be on the phone, calling 911.

Georges was already out of the car on his side, his attention riveted to the front door. "Something a little less messy than that."

She wasn't following him. At least, not mentally. She hurried up the walk behind him as he approached the front of her house. "Like what?"

He didn't answer her immediately. Instead, he took out his own keys. On the chain he also had two very thin pieces of metal no thicker than the lead used in a mechanical pencil. As she watched, he inserted both into the lock, keeping them at an angle to one another. He wiggled them around and she half expected him to say something like "Hocus-pocus" because, in less time than it took to observe what he was doing, Georges had opened her front door.

He gestured toward the interior of her house. "This," he replied, answering her question.

Rather than walk in, Vienna stared at him, a little confused about the kind of man she was with. "Is that your fallback career if this doctor thing doesn't work out for you?" she asked. "You're training to be a burglar?"

He grinned. "I hadn't thought about that, actually."

"Seriously," she pressed, "how did you manage to do that?" She'd seen it done in movies and on police dramas, but she thought that was just writers taking liberties with the truth. Apparently not.

He waited for her to walk in first. "I used to hang

out with the wrong crowd for a while—until Philippe yanked me out."

"Philippe?" They'd talked in the hospital, but mostly about her grandfather.

"My brother. My older brother," Georges added. And then, because he felt that he might as well give her the whole picture, he amended the label, even though there was nothing *half* about Philippe. "My older half brother."

The way he said it made her think there were more. "You have others?"

"Just one. Alain." Although he knew that his younger brother would take umbrage about the word *just* used to describe him. In his own way, Alain was every bit as flamboyant as their mother was. As blond as she was dark, Alain was the newly minted lawyer in the family, as well as playboy par excellence. There were times when the youngest of Lily Moreau's boys made him feel as if he were a saintly altar boy.

"Is he a half or a whole?"

He grinned. "A half."

Finally crossing the threshold, Vienna looked around. Nothing seemed to have changed. But it had. And it could have for the worst. What a difference a few hours made.

Trying to get her bearings, she turned around to face Georges. "Any sisters? Half or whole," she added for good measure.

"Not that I know of." Of course, what with two stepfathers and his own father in the mix, he could never be certain. None of the men had been monastic in nature. But no small voices, crying out in the wilderness had been heard from—so far. "At least, none that my mother had."

Vienna smiled. It had been so long, she hardly remembered what it felt like to have a mother. "Sounds like an interesting woman."

He could only laugh in response. "You don't know the half of it." When she raised an eyebrow, he said, "Maybe you've heard of her. Lily Moreau."

Vienna's mouth dropped open. "Of course I've heard of Lily Moreau." There'd been an article on her in a national magazine just last month. She'd read it in the dentist's office. "She's that wildly beautiful Bohemian artist. The one who says she always paints best when she's in love." She couldn't help staring at him, looking for similarities. "Lily Moreau is your *mother?*" she finally asked in disbelief.

He was used to getting that kind of a reaction. "When she can find the time to be," he replied with an air of someone who long ago had accepted the fact that his was not like all the other mothers. His burst in, larger than life, then disappeared in a flash, off to another showing, another gallery somewhere halfway around the world. Another man who promised to love her in exchange for basking in her aura. When he was younger, he'd resented both her lifestyle and her men, but eventually it no longer bothered him. She was just being Lily.

Vienna didn't know whether to envy him because of his famous mother or pity him for the same reason. It couldn't have been easy, having a personality as flamboyant as the celebrated artist as a mother, she thought. Aside from the recent article, Lily was in the news every so often, her paintings and her men earning almost equal lines of print.

"You seemed to have turned out all right." The words were uttered before she thought to hold them back. God, was that as judgmental-sounding as she thought? She hadn't meant it to be.

He grinned and inclined his head. "Except for the wild teen period," he allowed.

That had been his crossroads and it could have gone either way for him—had Philippe not physically wrestled him for possession of his confused soul the night he'd bailed him out of the local jail for shoplifting. Lily had found the lawyer who had gotten him off, but after that, Philippe was the one who had policed him like a newly paroled prisoner, making sure that he had no further contact with the boys who thought that robbing was a rite of passage and that eluding the police was the supreme challenge.

All his priorities and basic values had gotten reorganized that summer. It was also the last time the sound of approaching sirens had made him nervous.

Standing now within Vienna's small residence, Georges scanned the room. They were in the living room and he could see the kitchen just beyond. It was a nice, homey house, he thought. Something Lily would have instantly begun redecorating.

Love lived here. He could all but feel it permeating from the walls.

Turning around, he looked at the woman who had inadvertently caused him to take a mental stroll down memory lane and revisit the less-than-stellar portion of his past.

He had to be going. Even so, he was reluctant to leave her alone like this.

"You'll be all right now?" he asked her, his eyes holding hers.

His concern made her smile. Kindness was never unappreciated. "Believe it or not, I really can take care of myself."

"Didn't mean to imply that you couldn't." Even though she did stir protective feelings within him. He nodded toward the door. "I'll be going now."

She surprised him by placing her hand on his arm and detaining him. "I'll see you again, won't I?" He saw her catch her lower lip between her teeth, as if she felt she'd just made a blunder. "I mean, at the hospital. My grandfather—"

Vienna's voice trailed off. She had no idea how to finish the sentence gracefully without making it seem as if she were trying to corner him. The last thing she wanted in her life was any kind of male-female entanglement. Just that there was something about him that made her feel everything was going to be all right. And she needed to feel that.

Technically, the man wasn't his patient, he was Schulman's. But he was Schulman's surgical resident, so that made him part of the team. "I'll be looking in on him," Georges promised.

She breathed a sigh of relief. "I'd appreciate that." Vienna walked the three steps with him back to the front threshold. "Thanks again." She put out her hand and then, impulsively, as if deciding that wasn't personal enough, she suddenly dropped her hands, framed his face with them instead and kissed him.

It felt as if something magical had touched him. Just like the first time.

Georges caught himself wanting to extend the moment, the sensation. Wanting to sample a kiss in earnest, existing for its own sake rather than as an extension of her gratitude.

But that would be taking too much for granted. So he savored the brief, sweet contact and allowed her to back away.

"My pleasure," he murmured. And then he

left. As he made his way back to his car, he ran his tongue lightly along the outline of his lips. Sealing in her taste.

"Burning the firecracker at both ends again, Georges?"

The question came from his left. About to get back into his car after a quick shower and change of clothes, Georges had hurried by without realizing anyone was out yet.

He looked now toward the man standing several yards away from him, a newly fetched newspaper in his hand. Philippe raised the newspaper in a kind of salute.

Close as children, closer as adults, Georges and his two half brothers now lived in three separate houses built by a clever architect to look like one large, sprawling estate. One imposing door in the front, two on the opposite sides, all leading to different residences.

Philippe had the one in the middle, while he and Alain lived in the houses that flanked the central one. "Separate but equal" was what Philippe had said when he'd initially found the property. It was evident that Philippe still thought of himself as the patriarch and wanted to be close by in case he was needed.

It hadn't been a hard sell. Both he and Alain had liked the look of the houses and there was something subconsciously comforting about having your brothers close by, just not so close that they got into your business if you didn't want them to.

After graduating from medical school and four years into his residency at Blair Memorial Hospital, he would have thought that Philippe would have realized his little brother didn't need someone watching over him. Still, he supposed, old habits died hard. The parade of nannies notwithstanding, during their formative years Philippe had looked after both him and Alain when their mother was away, which was more than half the time.

Philippe was eyeing him now, waiting for some sort of a response.

Georges spread his hands innocently. Ordinarily, Philippe would be right. He did have a habit of going out after a grueling, endless shift. Some people recharged sleeping; he did it in the company of beautiful women. But not this time. At least, not exactly.

"Work-related," Georges told him.

Philippe moved closer. He made no attempt to hide the fact that he was giving him the once-over. "Dressed a little fancy for work, weren't you? I saw you come in earlier."

It struck him that in another life, Philippe might have made his living as an interrogator instead of the software genius he turned out to be. He saw no reason to lie. "I *was* on my way to see Diana."

Philippe nodded, as if he'd thought as much. Not

that he knew who Diana was, but Diana, Stella, Angela, it didn't matter. The names were all interchangeable. By the time one was learned, Georges had moved on. But it was always a woman who lured him out to play.

Amused, Philippe asked, "And that turned into work how?"

Georges shut his door. This might take a while. He had a few minutes to spare. "When a hit-and-run driver sideswiped the car behind me, trapping the passengers inside and sending the car spinning up against a hillside on PCH."

Philippe's eyes narrowed as he scrutinized his brother. He had no way of knowing that Georges' smoke-damaged clothing was stashed on the floor of his closet. But despite the time lapse and the shower, there was still the slight smell of smoke about Georges' dark hair. Knowing Georges, he wouldn't have hesitated when it came to saving lives.

"Anyone hurt?" Philippe asked, even as he continued to check Georges over for any indication that the hurt person might have been Georges himself.

Georges knew Philippe wouldn't be satisfied with a yes or no answer. His older brother might not talk much, but he expected his brothers to fill in the gaps.

"The man behind the wheel suffered a minor heart attack," he told Philippe. "The doors were sealed shut. I had to break a window to get inside and get him and his granddaughter out. I had her call Blair for an ambulance while I did CPR on the old man."

Philippe nodded, taking it all in. "How is he?"

"Fine now—so far," he qualified, then explained. "He needed emergency surgery."

Georges had mentioned that there'd been two people in the car. "And the girl?"

Georges wasn't aware that'd he frowned when he answered, but Philippe was. "A little banged up, but she refused to let herself be admitted. Stayed at the old man's side for most of the night."

"And you stayed by hers." It wasn't a guess. When it came to his brothers, Philippe had gotten good at filling in the blanks.

Georges nodded, then tried to sound modest as he added, "When I wasn't operating on her grandfather." There was no missing the pride in his voice.

Philippe looked at him with genuine surprise. He was aware that Georges routinely attended surgeries, but he didn't know that his brother was operating on patients. "They let you scrub in?"

Georges shrugged, doing his best to contain the excitement that scrubbing in as an assistant had generated. "They were short internal surgeons."

Philippe draped his arm around his brother's shoulders. "Sounds like you had a pretty eventful evening. Not as eventful as it might have been had you gone out with Diana," he surmised, teasing him, "but still, eventful. I take back what I was thinking."

Georges arched an eyebrow. "And what were you thinking?"

"That you're a hopeless playboy."

"Hey, we all can't be as steadfast as you, big brother. Zeroing in on one woman and pledging commitment without really taking the time to see what else is out there."

In direct contrast to their mother, Philippe seemed almost reclusive when it came to his social life, preferring the company of good friends to the dating field. But it was because he'd watched their mother go from relationship to relationship, all but fleeing when things became serious, that caused him to believe there was no use in searching for someone to spend his life with.

Until Janice and her bright-as-a-newly-minted-penny daughter had come into his life.

"I don't need to see what else is out there, Georges," Philippe informed him evenly, then smiled. "Some things you just know."

Georges folded his arms before him, waiting. "Like what?"

He wasn't one to profess love out loud, or make his feelings public. But loving Janice had changed some of that. "Like the fact that Janice is the one for me." He looked to see if his brother under-stood what he meant. "Janice is a once-in-a-lifetime woman."

Georges laughed at the sound of that. "Sounds like some kind of sect."

The best thing in the world that he could wish for Georges, for both his brothers, was to find someone like Janice. "It means, little brother, a woman like that comes along once in a man's lifetime and he had better be on his toes when she does. Because if he misses his chance, if he lets her slip through his fingers because he's too blind, he'll never see her like again. And the rest of his life could be spent looking for someone who even came close to her."

"Very poetic." Straightening, Georges unfolded his arms. He had to get going. "Don't get me wrong, Philippe. I think the world of Janice. Until she came along, Alain and I were afraid that you'd wind up some bitter old man we were going to have to share custody of. Sitting by the fire, rocking and uttering insane platitudes every so often." He grinned, clapping his brother on the back. "But now with Janice around, we don't have to worry anymore."

"Touching."

Georges was inclined to agree. "I thought so."

Philippe shifted, watching his brother open the driver's-side door. "So when are you planning on getting some sleep?"

Georges got in behind the wheel. "Don't worry, I have it penciled in for a week from Friday." He waved as he drove away.

But that was just the trouble, Philippe thought, heading back to his own house, he *did* worry. And would continue to do so until Georges found his own once-in-a-lifetime woman.

Chapter Seven

Georges was busy even before he entered the hospital. Parking his vehicle in the lot designated for hospital personnel—doctors had a closer lot, but he would not qualify for that until he completed his residency—he was about to walk through the main entrance when a woman stumbled right in front of him. He steadied her as best he could. She looked to be about ten months pregnant with a great deal to steady.

Helping her inside, he brought the woman to the admissions desk. English was not her first language. Because of the travels his mother had taken him and his brothers on, Georges knew a smattering of a handful of languages. Trying them out on the pregnant woman, they came together over French, enough so that he could put her at her ease and, more importantly, find out her name and the name of the doctor she was coming to see.

Once she was situated, Georges dashed over to the east wing, where he was supposed to have been on duty for the last half hour. His attending, John LaSalle, was not pleased about his being late and made no effort to hide the way he felt. But then Dr. Sheila Pollack, the head of the maternity ward, came by to personally thank him for helping with her patient. The woman's husband had been called and would be on his way in time for what appeared to be a very fast-track delivery.

After that, LaSalle retracted some of his harsher words, and Georges was left to take on his regular duties. Two more hours were eaten up.

He didn't get a chance to swing by Amos Schwarzwalden's room on the third floor until just a little before eleven.

Georges knocked softly in order not to disturb the man if he was still asleep. Opening the door, he saw that the old man was not alone. Her back to the door, his granddaughter was sitting beside Schwarz-walden's bed, just as she had been last night.

Vienna twisted around in her chair to see who

opened the door. The smile that greeted him instantly spread warmth all through his chest.

Her hair was piled up on her head and pinned haphazardly, with tendrils descending here and there. She looked younger somehow, more vulnerable now than she had last night, he thought.

Coming into the room, he caught the scent of something warm and tempting. He would have said it was her, but there was a dash of cinnamon mixed in. He doubted that she dabbed cinnamon behind her ears.

That was when he saw the open white box at the foot of her grandfather's bed. Streamers of entwining blue and pink were embossed on the sides, obviously a logo of some sort. The box was crammed full with pastries.

Fresh from the oven from the smell of it, he thought.

Vienna rose to her feet and crossed to him. "Hi." Was it possible for a single word to all but vibrate with sunshine? he wondered. "He's still unconscious," she told him needlessly.

"Not unusual," he assured her. "His body needs the time to heal. This is the best way. Don't worry, your grandfather'll come around." He glanced at the open box. She'd probably brought that so he would see something familiar when he opened his eyes, Georges surmised. Too bad. "But when he does, he really can't have those right now."

"I know." Picking up the box, she presented it to him. "I made them for you."

He held the box as if he meant to pass it back to her. "Me?"

Her smile grew wider as she nodded. "I'm not as good as my grandfather," she freely admitted, "but he did teach me a few things." Very gently, she pushed the box back toward him. "It's just my way of saying thank you—other than paying the bill." Her eyes were shining with humor and it took effort to draw his own away.

When he did, Georges gazed down at the box in his hands. There had to be over a dozen assorted pastries and cakes in it, maybe more. Each looked lighter and more delectable than the last.

Ever since he was a little boy, he'd never been one to stop for a morning meal. That was because he was never hungry before noon, no matter what time he got up. Breakfast for him these days was an extra-large container of coffee. Caffeine rather than nutrition saw him through his morning hours. A bad attitude for a doctor, he knew, but he had yet to run up against the age-old saying of, "Physician, heal thyself."

However, there was something about the box of mouthwatering confections that prompted him to take a small sample. Breaking off a tiny piece of one, he popped it into his mouth. Once he did, he wanted more.

The experience was not unlike his reaction to Vienna's kiss last night. Or had that been this morning? The hours were running together for him at this point, and he'd lost his markings.

But his memory was sharp when it came to remembering the impact.

"Good," he murmured with enthusiasm, licking a drop of frosting from his index finger.

"Of course she is good."

The reedy-sounding affirmation came from the patient in the bed. Georges and Vienna looked at each other, wide-eyed, before approaching the man in the bed.

"She is my granddaughter." Amos's eyes all but disappeared as he smiled at her. "Everything she does is good."

Georges nodded. The comment seemed to come out on its own. "I have no doubt."

Vienna hardly heard him. Her heart hammered very loudly in her ears. "Grandpa, you're awake." Overjoyed, she took his hand and pressed a kiss to it, careful not to dislodge any of the lines attached to him.

"Why shouldn't I be awake? The sun is up." And then he became aware of his present surroundings.

Amos frowned at the various tethers he saw attached to his body. Two different IVs ran into his arm, one for nutrition, one for medication, as well as a clear tube beneath his nose supplementing his oxygen. A wide cuff was wrapped around his other arm, periodically measuring his blood pressure, heartbeat and various other vital signs.

"Why am I tied down like this?" he asked Vienna. Then he turned toward the man he didn't recognize. Maybe he had an explanation for all this. "What have I done?"

Vienna fought back tears of joy. She feathered her fingertips along the old man's finely lined brow, lightly brushing back his hair. "Nothing, Grandpa. You've lived. Survived."

"Do you remember anything that happened, sir?" Georges asked. It was not uncommon for people involved in an accident not to remember anything for several hours, sometimes days, after the accident.

Amos paused for a long moment, as if to scan the depths of his mind for a scrap of information that somehow didn't belong there. But in the end, he slowly moved his head from side to side.

"No," he confessed and it looked as if the admission troubled him. "What is it I should be remembering?"

Vienna wrapped her hand about her grandfather's, as if to temporarily give him her strength. He'd always been her rock. Now it was time to return the favor.

"There was an accident, Grandpa. A drunk driver hit us. The Pontiac spun out and wound up hitting the side of hill."

The news had him clutching her hand harder as he scrutinized her face. "You? You are hurt?"

She smiled. He always thought of her first, never himself. "No, Grandpa, I'm not." She nodded toward Georges. "Thanks to Dr. Armand."

The lines in his forehead became more pronounced as Amos's frown deepened. "I don't understand."

Georges left the explanation up to her. He had a feeling that the old man would understand it better if it came from Vienna.

"He saw the accident and risked his life to save ours. He got me out of the car and then dragged you out." Her voice quivered just a little as she added, "You had a heart attack."

Amos's face was immobile. "No."

"Yes," she contradicted gently. "You did. Dr. Armand gave you CPR and then had the ambulance bring you here." Her eyes shifted to the man's chest. Amos wore the customary hospital gown assigned to everyone, but that didn't keep her from visualizing the long, fresh surgical cuts beneath. "You had to have emergency surgery."

"All this and I do not remember?" Uttered in awe, it was a question, an appeal to both her and the man beside her to help him recall the events.

Very lightly, she ran the back of her knuckles along his cheek. A tad of his color was returning, she thought with relief.

"You were unconscious, Grandpa. But now you're back. And I'm ever so grateful." She shifted her eyes toward Georges to underscore her feelings before she looked back at her grandfather again.

Amos nodded slowly, trying to assimilate the information coming at him. He raised his eyes to her face. "What about the car?"

"Gone," she told him. "It burst into flames just as Georges got you out."

"Georges?"

"Dr. Armand," Vienna corrected herself.

She'd lapsed just then. The man's profession demanded that respect be accorded him. And yet, after all they had been through in such a short space of time, it didn't seem quite right being so formal. He'd given both her grandfather and her their lives back.

"I see." The words left Amos's lips in slow motion. "We'll need a new one."

"Yes, we will." She smiled at him fondly, her heart feeling so full she could barely breathe. Was there ever a time when her grandfather didn't look forward, didn't push toward the future rather than lament the past? He was going to be just fine, she assured herself.

"What about the shop?" Amos realized suddenly. He attempted to sit up. "I should be there."

"You should be here." With gentle but firm hands, she pushed her grandfather back onto the bed. "Raul is in the back, baking. Zelda is in the front, taking care of the customers. Everything's running smoothly for now." Vienna looked at the old man pointedly, not about to stand for an argument. She could be tough if she had to be. He had taught her that. "We all just want you to get better."

Georges had stood off to the side, feeling that the old man needed this, needed to have his grand-daughter refresh his parameters for him and help him orient himself. He sensed it would make the man feel better and ultimately be more cooperative when it came to his treatment.

But now it was his turn. He had rounds to make with Schulman soon, and he didn't want to miss this opportunity to check out Amos's condition before he had to get on with his work.

So he came now to stand by the man's bed, doing his best not to seem threatening in any way. There were people who had almost a pathological fear of doctors. "How do you feel, Mr. Schwarzwalden?"

Amos leaned back against his pillows and exhaled dramatically. "Like elephants have been dancing on my body." He slanted a look at the younger man and smiled. "And please, you saved my granddaughter. Call me Amos."

Georges inclined his head, smiling back. "All right, Amos." He got down to business, keeping in mind that he didn't want to alarm his patient. "These elephants, do you feel like they're pressing on your chest?"

Amos considered the question and watched Vienna, who was holding her breath, waiting for him to answer. "No, all over."

Then it wasn't his heart, Georges thought. Just a general achiness, which was to be expected. Had the pain been isolated to the man's chest area, it could have been an indication that more heart trouble needed to be addressed.

Picking up the chart, Georges made several notations before resting it on the bed. Rather than rely strictly on the machine readings, he checked over Amos's vital signs on his own. Measuring his blood pressure, taking his pulse, listening to his heart and lungs.

Finished, because he had verified it for himself, he felt a sense of relief at the outcome.

"Your pupils are fine," he told Amos, shutting off the light he'd shone into the man's eyes. "No indications of a concussion. Your heartbeat is strong, your blood pressure remarkably low for a man your age."

The grin on Amos's face was completely reminiscent of his granddaughter's expression. "That is because I am not a man my age, Doctor. I am a man much younger than my age."

Vienna felt she needed to explain that to Georges

before he thought that her grandfather was lapsing into some sort of childish babble.

"Grandpa believes that everyone has to get older, but no one has to get old." It was a saying Amos attributed to the late comedian George Burns. Her grandfather had made it his own, repeating it as often as he felt was necessary. She secretly felt that it was more of a case of self-hypnosis than anything else because he certainly was a true believer these days.

Georges grinned, retiring his stethoscope. "Great philosophy to have." He looked at the pastry chef. "I think you'd get along very well with my mother."

Despite his condition, interest seemed to instantly pique on Amos's face. "She is single, your mother?" he asked.

Georges thought of the man currently squiring his mother around. Kyle something-or-other. A would-be artist some twenty-five years younger than Lily. She claimed being with Kyle made her feel like a schoolgirl again. He'd always believed in live and let live, but he had to admit that he and his brothers were not happy about this one. His mother had brought him around several times, secretly, he was certain, seeking their approval.

But much as he didn't like the way she was running her life lately, it was her life and he had no right to interfere. "Not at the moment."

Amos has a keen ear. He dispensed advice along

with his baked goods at his store every day. "Oh? It does not sound as if you approve of this person in your mother's life."

Georges shrugged casually, as if he really didn't have a hard-and-fast opinion on the matter. "She's done better."

"His mother is Lily Moreau," Vienna interjected for her grandfather's benefit.

"Lily Moreau?" Complete surprise and then keen interest washed across Amos Schwarzwalden's still very pale complexion. "The famous artist?"

"One and the same," Georges replied with a weariness that caught him off guard. He hadn't meant to sound like that when admitting to their connection.

Try as he might, Georges couldn't remember a single time when someone didn't instantly know who his mother was when her name came up in the conversation. Most of the time, he was proud of her, proud of her work and even of her Bohemian bravado. But lately, he found himself wishing she would settle down again. Just not with someone young enough to be her son.

"You must bring her to the shop," Amos told him with enthusiasm, then added with a resigned note, "Once you let me go back to it."

He wasn't about to fall for that sorrowful face, Georges thought. He had a feeling Amos could get people to do what he wanted. He was one of those endearing people you hated saying no to.

"That all depends on you, Mr.—ah, Amos," Georges stopped, correcting himself. And then, because the man's attitude seemed so positive, he gave him something to be positive about. He gave him the good news. "But if you keep going the way you are, I don't see any reason why we won't be discharging you in a few days."

"A few days?" Amos echoed. Rather than be happy, the old man seemed somewhat disheartened. "I was hoping to be released in a few hours."

"You had a lot of internal injuries, Amos. Ruptured spleen, bruised liver, cracked ribs." He didn't bother mentioning the heart attack. He didn't want the man to feel overwhelmed. It was enough that they all knew one had happened. "You need time to heal. We just want to make sure everything's mending properly before we set you loose again." Removing the stethoscope from around his neck, he put it in his deep pocket. "Why don't you take this opportunity to rest. According to what your granddaughter says, you haven't had a vacation in years."

Amos laughed under his breath. "No disrespect, Doctor, but this is not exactly a place I would choose to have my vacation."

Neither would he, Georges thought. "Luck of the draw, Amos, luck of the draw." Closing the chart, he hung it off the foot of the bed again. "I'll stop by later to look in on you again," he promised.

Amos nodded, looking less than happy about the scenario. "Unfortunately, I will be here."

"You'd better believe it," Vienna told her grandfather with feeling.

"I raised her to be tough," Amos confided to Georges. And then he frowned as he looked at Vienna again. "Perhaps that was not such a good move."

Georges couldn't help the admiring grin that rose to his lips as he eyed the man's granddaughter one last time. The word *knockout* ran through his mind. "It was from where I'm standing."

"I like him," Amos told Vienna the moment the door was closed again and Georges had left.

Absently, Vienna agreed. "So do I."

Despite his condition, Amos was instantly alert. "Oh?"

She could read him like a book, an old, beloved, well-read book. "Get that look out of your eye, Grandpa. I meant as a doctor."

The smile on his lips was positively mischievous. "I didn't." He gave her a long, penetrating look. "It is about time you forgot all about that Edward person. He was not worthy of you."

He'd get no argument from her, not after the final scene between them. She didn't do well with ultimatums, and Edward had made it clear that she had to choose—her grandfather or him. It wasn't a fair contest. Edward hadn't even come close—because her grandfather would have never asked her to choose between them.

"You're right, he wasn't. But I'm not looking to replace him right now." She took her grandfather's hand in hers. "All I want right now is for you to get better." Her eyes misted as she said, "I don't know what I'd do if anything ever happened to you."

"You would continue, Vienna. You are strong. Like your mother was, and her mother before her." It was a source of pride within the family that the women on the family tree were made of un-bendable mettle. "But," he went on to allow, "it does not hurt to have someone in your life who is looking out for you."

How had they circled back to this? "Stop right there," Vienna warned him. "If that someone isn't you, I don't want to talk about it."

He sighed, resigned. For now. "Very well. Tell me about the shop."

His mistress, Vienna thought fondly. Her grandfather loved the shop the way few men loved their wives. "The customers all want to know where you are."

The questions about what had happened had come so steadily from his crowd of regulars that she's stopped to print up a short, detailed account of the accident and posted it on the outside door. All it had done was generate more questions. Which was why it had taken her so long to get here.

"They all send their good wishes for a speedy recovery."

Amos smiled, pleased. "That is nice." And then he looked at her intently, sobering. "You are sure that you are all right? That you were not hurt?"

"I'm sure. Georges insisted on checking me out last night."

He nodded knowingly. "And this checking out, it was nice for you?"

Vienna laughed and shook her head. "As a doctor, Grandpa, he checked me out as a doctor."

"I saw the way he looked at you when he was here. Not just as a doctor, Vienna, but as a man. Men know these things," he informed her solemnly. "And this I can tell you, he is a nice man, to risk his life for strangers."

Not that she was playing devil's advocate, but she really didn't want her grandfather making something out of nothing. "He's a doctor, Grandpa. He's supposed to help people."

"In the hospital or his office, yes," he agreed. "Burning cars are another story." And then, before she could say anything to counter him, Amos sighed. He seemed to fade into the bed. "I am tired right now, Vienna. Maybe I should rest, like he said."

"Maybe," she agreed fondly.

Her grandfather was asleep before the second syllable had faded away.

Chapter Eight

"**Y**ou're a big hit with the nurses," Georges told Vienna when she walked out of her grandfather's room a few minutes later.

He'd purposely hung around the area, taking his time finishing up a chart just in case she ventured out of the room. But she was holding her purse, which meant she was leaving. That surprised him. After the way she'd kept vigil at her grandfather's side last night and early this morning, he hadn't expected her to be leaving so soon. He wondered where she was going. And when he would see her again.

Vienna eyed him quizzically and he realized that

he had gotten ahead of himself again. It was a habit he'd picked up from his mother. His mind was always moving, juggling a hundred thoughts at once. Sometimes, when he spoke, it was in the middle of a thought. He backtracked now.

"The pastries you brought," he explained. The box he nodded at was completely empty. "I believe the consensus was that they were 'to die for.'"

"Oh." She glanced down at the empty box. Because neatness was ingrained in her, she picked it up and flattened out the sides, then dropped it into the wastebasket she saw by the side of the desk. "I thought you'd take them home and eat them yourself." If she'd known that he was going to pass them around, she would have brought more.

"That's just the trouble, I would have." He patted his middle, which was flat by design, not through an accident of nature. "And then I'd have to buy a whole new wardrobe."

"No, you wouldn't. That's my grandfather's secret." Other ingredients were substituted for the more fattening ones, drastically reducing the caloric composition of the pastries he prepared. "His pastries aren't as fattening as you think they are."

She began to move toward the elevators and he fell into step with her. "Eating twelve of anything at one sitting is fattening," he assured her. "You're leaving already?"

Glancing at her watch out of habit, she nodded. "Have to." Losing her purse in the fire had created a lot of time-consuming, annoying problems for her. She'd had to call and order replacements for her credit cards. But that wasn't the worst of it. "I can't rent a car until I can show the rental agency my driver's license, and I don't have a driver's license to show them until I can get it replaced. Which means—" she sighed "—I have to go and wait in some endless line at the DMV. Meanwhile, I'm stuck calling cab companies." Reaching the elevators, she pressed the Down button.

Georges suddenly thought of a way out for her. "Do you have a cab waiting for you in the parking lot?" he asked.

Vienna shook her head. She was going to call one when she got to the lobby. "Not yet."

The elevator arrived, but he drew her aside. "Why don't you hang on a second?"

She followed him gamely over to the side of the corridor. "What do you have in mind?" His smile told her that maybe she'd just asked a loaded question.

Banking down the first response that rose to his lips, he went with a far safer one as he took out his cell phone from the depths of his pocket. "I might be able to pull a few strings to keep you from having to wait in that endless DMV line."

The thought of *not* having to spend the next two

hours shifting from side to side and occasionally moving forward on a spiraling DMV line sounded like heaven. "You know someone?"

"Technically, my cousin Remy knows someone." Georges flashed her a reassuring smile as he pressed a number on his keypad and then placed the phone to his ear. "But I know my cousin Remy, so, by association, yes, I know someone."

"But will he—"

She didn't get a chance to complete her question. His cousin had obviously come on the other end. Georges had raised his hand, indicating that she should refrain from saying anything further.

Five minutes later, after asking her a few questions and passing the answers to his cousin, giving the man all the necessary information, it was settled. Remy had assured him that a copy of Vienna Hollenbeck's original driver's license would be messengered to her house by late afternoon.

When he told her, Vienna thought it was nothing short of a miracle. But then, she was beginning to think Georges Armand was in the business of miracles. "I didn't think you could do that."

He winked, slipping the phone back into his pocket. "There are ways around a great many things if you just take the trouble to find the right path."

Her grandfather had taught her to be a dreamer, but there was a practical bent to her, as well. Whenever possible, she tried to be prepared for all contingencies. "But what if his friend finds he can't get a copy of my license?"

Georges glanced down at the pocket where he'd deposited his cell phone. "If that rings in the next few minutes, then Remy's friend hit a snag. If it doesn't, you're home free."

She eyed his pocket, then raised her eyes to his face. "I must say, you certainly are a handy man to have around."

When she looked at him like that, he could feel the very breath stopping in his lungs. He'd never had anyone look at him quite like that before. It took him a second to get his wits back about him.

"I have my moments."

Now there was an understatement, she thought. How was she ever going to pay this man back? Crossing back to the elevators, she pressed the Down button again.

"I just keep slipping deeper and deeper into your debt."

He moved so that she could look at him. "Have dinner with me and we'll call it even."

Dinner. That wouldn't make them even by a long shot. But it would open a door she wasn't sure if she wanted to open.

"Dr. Armand, Dr. Schulman is looking for you," a nurse called out to him as she came down the corridor from the nurses' station. "He was just called down to the E.R. and he wants you there to evaluate a patient."

Georges knew better than to stall, even for a moment. Blair was a teaching hospital, and he was still a student. If he wanted to do well here, he couldn't afford to get on the wrong side of the surgeon.

"Thank you." The elevator arrived just then. "I'll ride down with you," he said to Vienna.

But to his surprise, she stepped back. "I forgot something in my grandfather's room."

The doors began to close. "Dinner?" he pressed, placing his hand between the doors to keep them from shutting before he got his answer.

But she was already hurrying down the corridor back to her grandfather's room. "I'll get back to you," she promised, throwing the words over her shoulder.

The next moment, the elevator doors closed and he was gone. Vienna stopped. Watching the doors for a second, she retraced her steps back to the elevator bank. She let out a long, ragged breath as she pressed the Down button for the third time.

There was no denying that she would have loved nothing more than to say yes to the doctor's invitation. But that was just the problem. She would have *loved* to. And that was dangerous. There was something about Dr. Georges Armand, something that pulled at her, something that, at the same time, warned her that if she said yes to his invitation, that if she met him outside the protective four walls of the hospital, she would wind up getting involved with him. Passionately.

The last thing she wanted right now was to get involved with someone, passionately or otherwise. Her grandfather needed her. And she needed to sort out her life, which still felt as if it were a shambles despite the structure she'd given it lately. She'd put her whole heart and soul into caring for the wrong man. Coming to that realization had shaken her up. It made her doubt her instincts, at least her instincts when it came to making any sound judgments about men.

There was no denying that the sight of Georges' wicked smile made her heart flutter in double time, but acting on that might have some consequences attached to it. She had no room for serious heartache. For the time being, she just wanted to purge any and all memories of Edward and go on with her life. Slowly.

Something told her that if she went out with Georges, tempting though it was, things would proceed at a rate far from languid and slow.

This was a lot better, she thought, stepping into the elevator. The nurse had interrupted them just in time, sparing her from having to turn Georges down. She didn't want to hurt him; she just didn't want to be hurt herself.

Arriving on the first floor, Vienna fished out the phone number of the taxicab company she'd copied down before leaving for the bakery this morning. Since Georges had rescued her from having to endure the DMV, she needed to get back to the bakery to make sure that Raul hadn't let his temperament get the better of him. Raul and Zelda got into it over some trivial thing almost every day.

Love had to be in the air, she mused, walking over to a lone public phone.

Georges made it a rule never to push. Pursue, yes, but never push. If he had to wear a woman down to get her to say yes, then it wasn't worth it. God knew that practically from the day he was born, he'd all but had to beat women off with a stick and he never lacked for companionship. All he had to do was smile and there would be willing women beside him. It was just the way things were.

When he was barely a teenager, Lily had laughed and said she was afraid that he might become a professional ladies' man. But Philippe had kept after him, always making him mindful of his potential and the real need, since family and position were merely an accident of birth, for the *haves* to give a little something back to the *have-nots*.

But his philosophy notwithstanding, Georges caught himself wanting to push. Wanting to convince Vienna to have dinner with him. Because he had a feeling that once they broke bread together, other pleasing events would follow naturally.

And he wanted them to follow.

Wanted to discover what the texture of her skin felt like beneath his fingertips. Wanted to explore all the different tastes and flavors that went into making up this particular woman.

It had been five days since he'd first met her. Four days since he'd suggested dinner. Their paths crossed regularly in her grandfather's room, but she said nothing to indicate that she wanted to take him up on his offer. So he didn't offer again.

But he wanted to.

She'd infiltrated his mind, something that never happened. Oh, he thought about women, thought about them a great deal, but only when he wanted to. Their faces did not suddenly come, unbidden, materializing before his mind's eye.

Hers did. He had no idea what to make of it. Or what to do.

Georges frowned as he sat at the circular table at his older brother's weekly card game, completely oblivious to the cards he was holding. His thoughts were drifting again. And they were drifting toward the blonde who hadn't taken him up on his invitation.

What the hell did all this mean?

"Fold," he heard his cousin Vinnie Mirabeau,

who sat opposite him, announce just as he dropped his cards facedown on the table. Vinnie pinned him with a knowing look. "You're doing that on purpose, but I'm not falling for it."

Roused, Georges eyed him curiously. He hadn't a clue what Vinnie was going on about. "It?"

"Making that face," Remy chimed it, following suit and tossing his cards down. "Like you don't like what you see. You don't have a poker face, Georges. Everything you think is normally right there, but even you know better than to frown at your cards. So if you're frowning, that means you're trying to put one over on us because you've got one hell of a hand."

Philippe laughed, shaking his head at Remy. "I think you're overthinking this and giving him way too much credit. Georges is preoccupied. His eyes weren't even on his cards when he frowned."

That was a little too close to home. Not to mention insulting. "Georges is right here, you know," Georges pointed out, looking at his older brother. "You don't have to talk about me as if I were some cardboard place holder you stuck on a chair."

"True," Alain allowed good-naturedly. "A cardboard place holder might present more of a challenge." He flashed a confident smile. "I'll see your ten and raise you five more," he told Georges.

Alain counted out a total of fifteen toothpicks,

some yellow, some blue, the different colors designating different point values rather than different dollar amounts.

They never played for money, Philippe made sure of that. His father, Jon Zabelle, Lily's first husband, had been a reckless gambler, hopelessly addicted to any and every game of chance ever created. He very nearly cost Lily everything she had until she put a stop to it by putting a stop to their marriage.

Suspecting he'd been bitten by the gambling bug, as well, Philippe sought to assuage his urges to bet by hosting this game and playing for the big win— which amounted to the big loser of the week having to do chores of some sort for the big winner. Chores varied with the winner, but no one had complained so far. At least, not genuinely. A little bit of griping was expected.

The poker game was a weekly affair that usually took place in Philippe's house and included all three brothers, as well as an assortment of cousins and friends who came and went from the table. Exchange of conversation and information was always the most valued by-product of the evening.

Gordon, Janice's older brother and his soon-to-be-brother-in-law, sighed as he tossed in his own hand. There weren't too many toothpicks left in his personal pile. "This is getting too rich for my blood. All I've got is a pair of sixes."

Philippe's expression was solemn and completely unreadable as he nodded. Looking around at the faces about his table, he asked, "Any more bets?" Everyone but Georges and Alain had dropped out.

Alain was the picture of confidence as he glanced down at his cards. "Nope."

"Not me," Georges replied.

It was time to end this. "Okay, I call." Philippe looked at his youngest brother first. "What have you got?"

Alain grinned and shrugged. It was obvious that he'd been hoping to bluff his way through. He laid his cards on the table. "Three of a kind," he answered, grouping his three jacks together.

"Too bad, I have a straight," Philippe told Alain.

Georges raised his eyes in surprise. "Me, too," he announced.

Remy laughed as he shook his head. "Put 'em down, boys," he prompted. "Let's see whose straight's the higher one." Philippe and Georges put their cards down at the same time. Looking from one set of cards to the other, Remy snorted, then hit the back of Georges' head with the side of his hand the way he used to when they were boys together. "Dummy, that's a straight flush you have."

Georges blinked, looking down at the cards as if this was the first time he was seeing them. He was every bit as preoccupied as Philippe had pointed out. "Oh, yeah, I guess it is." Raising his eyes to look around the table, he couldn't resist asking, "Does that mean that I win?"

"No, that means we'll just let you hold on to the toothpicks for tonight," Alain retorted in momentary disgust. "I say, if he doesn't know he's won, he doesn't deserve to win." But since that didn't hit a responsive chord with Philippe, Alain sighed and shook his head. Then he looked at Georges more closely. "Just where the hell are you tonight?"

Nowhere he wanted to admit, Georges thought ruefully. So he merely shrugged as he gathered together the colorful slivers of wood and drew them over to the pile he already had in front of him.

"Just a little off my game, so to speak," he said, addressing his answer to the table in general. "Had a tough case today at the hospital." It was a good, all-purpose excuse, one that he felt wouldn't be questioned by the others.

Vinnie snorted at the revelation. "And that, ladies and gentlemen, is why I don't trust hospitals." He glanced toward Georges. "Doctors are always rethinking their decisions."

"Well, in your case," Georges commented cheerfully, "they're probably just trying to figure out the best way to treat whatever it is you are." His humor returned as he successfully banked down any further teeth-jarring thoughts of bright blue eyes and a wide, inviting mouth that pulled into a smile all too easily. A mouth that kept tempting him every time he thought about it.

About her.

About kissing her.

An uneasy edginess threatened to recapture him. This wasn't like him, all but mooning over a woman. He never let thoughts of *any* woman interfere with either his work or the downtime he spent with his brothers and cousins. It was as if something had short-circuited inside of him.

"Well, while you're thinking, how about we play another hand?" Remy asked, gathering the cards together and shuffling them. It was his turn to deal. "Or is that too much multitasking for you?"

Georges watched as Remy all but made the cards dance for him. Of all of them, he was the handiest when it came to cards. "Just shut up and deal. I'm feeling lucky."

"Oh, what's her name?" Alain laughed as he turned to look at Georges.

"Never mind, don't tell us," Vinnie begged. "It'll be someone else by next week. I've given up trying to keep track of you and Alain over here." And then he looked over at their host. "Philippe here has the right idea. Find yourself one decent woman and settle down."

"You're only saying that because you can't even find one," Alain responded.

"Well, if you and Georges weren't systematically trying to go through the entire female population of Southern California, the rest of us might get a break," Remy responded.

"Speak for yourself, Remy," Vinnie told his cousin. "Me, I'm doing just fine." And then he grinned. "I hear congratulations are in order, Philippe."

"They are?" Georges looked at Philippe. "Why?"

"He'd making an honest woman of Janice," Vinnie replied, then slanted a glance toward Gordon. "No offense, Gordon."

"None taken. That's great news, Philippe. About time, too," Gordon added. "J.D. could stand to have some happiness in her life."

"What makes you think Philippe's going to do that?" Alain asked. "Trust me, I lived with the guy for eighteen years. He didn't make me happy."

Philippe blew out a breath. "Just be happy I let you live. Now, are we going to play poker, or are we going to sit around like a bunch of useless old men and gossip?" he asked.

"I'm dealing," Remy declared obediently. "I'm dealing."

Philippe nodded as he began to pick up the cards that were coming his way. "That's better," he murmured in approval.

Chapter Nine

Amos Schwarzwalden frowned. It wasn't an expression ordinarily seen on his jovial face. He watched his examining physician remove the stethoscope from his ears.

Amos sighed sadly. "And here I thought I liked you, boy."

Georges smiled. He made no attempt to correct his patient, or point out that he had not been a "boy" in a very long while. At Amos's age, he surmised the man thought of everyone under the age of fifty as young enough to merit the label of "boy" or "girl." Besides, he could well understand the man's disappointment. In his place, he would be tugging at the invisible restraints, eager to leave the second he was conscious. He knew the good that could be accomplished at a hospital, but psychologically, as Dorothy had once chanted, there was no place like home.

"I'm sorry," Georges apologized with feeling, "but this is really for your own good."

Amos's frown deepened until it seemed etched in. "Keeping me here instead of letting me go home? How is that for my good?"

"Well, there is that code blue incident," he needlessly reminded him. It had transpired just as he was about to go off duty last night. At the elevator, about to get in, he heard the alarm sound and somehow just *knew* it was Vienna's grandfather. He'd run all the way back to the room. One application of the paddles and the man's heart regained its rightful rhythm. Luckily, Vienna hadn't been there to witness any of that. "You gave us quite a scare." Slipping the stethoscope from his neck, he put it in his pocket. "Your heart stopped beating again. We need to know why."

Amos seemed completely unfazed as he shrugged his wide shoulders. "That is simple," he told Georges. "It doesn't like the food here. Let me go home and everything will be fine."

There wasn't a chance in hell that the man was going to leave today. Not unless Amos tied the bed sheets together and slipped out through one of the windows. "I'm afraid we need the pleasure of your company for another day, Amos."

Amos eyed him closely. "Just one more day, then? And then I'm free?"

Georges knew better than to promise. He made one last notation on the man's chart, then replaced it at the edge of the bed. "With luck. If your tests all come back negative—"

Amos shook his head, amused. "I am seventy-four years old, boy. The tests won't be negative. At seventy-four, there is *always* something wrong. All they need to be is better than the next seventy-four-year-old's tests."

"He's just thinking of you, Grandpa."

Georges turned around and saw that Vienna had come into the room. She looked like sunshine, he thought, feeling a warmth materializing out of nowhere to wrap itself around him.

Amos laughed, shaking his head as he waved away the thought. "Let him think a little more about you and less about me."

Embarrassed, Vienna gave her grandfather a warning look that should have silenced him. "Grandpa."

Think more about her? Georges' brain echoed. Not possible. This last week alone, Vienna had been on his mind to the exclusion of everyone else in his life. Thoughts of her had infiltrated his mind to the point that it almost got in the way of his work.

Not something he was accustomed to, Georges thought. It gave him more than a little concern. He figured the only way he was going to get past this was to make love with her and put it all behind him. Once the exhilarating thrill of the hunt was gone, things would start getting back to normal for him.

"I'm sorry," she apologized without looking in Georges' direction. He noted that her complexion looked a little rosier than it had a moment earlier. "My grandfather tends to be a little blunt at times."

"I do not hide what is on my mind, if that is what you mean," Amos told his granddaughter. His eyes shifted toward Georges. His eyes, Georges thought, were almost as hypnotic as hers. "That would be a waste of time and I do not know how much longer I have." His eyes locked with Georges'. "I want to be sure there is someone to look out for Vienna."

Okay, enough was enough. In another minute, he was going to be accepting offers of beads and horses in trade for her.

"Grandpa," she admonished fondly, "women don't need men to look out for them anymore."

"Of course they do," Amos told her matter-of-factly in that voice the didn't allow for any argument. Before she could refute his words, he said, "Just like men need women to look after them." He turned toward the only other person in the room with them. "Am I right, Georges?"

He wanted to beg off before he was drawn into a family argument, however calmly advanced it might be. But something inside of him had him agreeing with the old man's philosophy. So he smiled at Vienna and said, "Sounds about right to me."

Her eyes met his. There was that wariness again in them despite the easy smile on her lips.

"You don't have to humor him," she told Georges. "Lord knows, I do plenty of that on my own."

He had no doubt. Amos Schwarzwalden looked to be a lovable man, but he also struck him as someone who wasn't easily manipulated and could stick to his guns if need be.

He wondered if that ran in the family.

"Could I see you for a moment?" Georges asked Vienna.

She seemed surprised by the request and then nodded. "Sure."

"If he tries to talk you into agreeing to make me stay here longer than tomorrow," Amos called out to her, raising his voice, "the answer is no."

"Yes, Grandpa," she returned patiently. She picked her battles carefully and never raced into the field prematurely. If her grandfather had to stay in the hospital longer than tomorrow, then tomorrow was time enough to let him know about that.

Right now, she was curious as to what the doctor wanted to tell her away from her grandfather's bedside. Instincts told her it had nothing to do with the man's health.

Georges drew her aside right outside the door. He kept his back to the corridor, creating their personal pocket of space. "You never gave me an answer."

Vienna raised her eyes innocently to his. "To?"

She was stalling, he thought. And right there, that should have been his answer. But something within him resisted. He didn't want to take no as her final decision. "Having dinner with me."

A smile teased the corners of the mouth she tried vainly to keep straight. "Didn't I?"

"I was called away before you could give me an answer," he reminded her.

She pretended to remember. In reality, the scenario had never been far from her thoughts. She didn't know whether to view it as an opportunity she'd let slip away, or a bullet she had dodged. Because something told her that in the sum total of things, any time she spent with this man was going to matter.

"Oh, that's right. You had to hurry off to a patient."

She wasn't fooling him for a second. She hadn't forgotten, he thought. "And what were you about to say just before I 'hurried off?'" he prodded, then, to forestall a negative response, he quickly added,

"Now before you answer, let me just tell you that dinner can be anywhere you choose. In the middle of Huntington Gardens if you want." Just in case she was afraid he'd come on to her—which he very much wanted to, but at the same time, knew he could hold himself in check indefinitely. "I would just very much like to have dinner with you."

Oh God, me, too.

She knew she was in trouble. "Why?" she pressed. Humor curved her mouth, but her eyes were serious, probing. Maybe he'd say something to turn her off and then she'd be safe instead of feeling as if she were sinking. Quickly.

"Because I like your company," he told her simply. "I like talking to you. Here," he volunteered, holding his hand out to her. "Touch me. See if there's an ulterior motive. See if you don't find that saying yes isn't a mistake."

When she made no move to place her hand on his, he did it for her, placing her hand on top of his.

Touched, amused, Vienna smiled as she shook her head. "It doesn't work that way," she reminded him. "I told you, I'm not clairvoyant. I just get…feelings…sometimes." And boy, were there feelings rumbling through her now. But none of them were her usual kind—like the one that begged Georges to be in the operating room with her grandfather.

His eyes held hers. "And you have no feelings about me?"

Her knees felt funny, as did her stomach. "That isn't quite accurate," she allowed, the words leaving her lips slowly.

"Oh?"

The smile that curved his lips found its target immediately. Her queasy stomach swiftly acquired knots that stole her breath.

She forced herself to sound calm and in control. It was her only hope. "Dr. Armand, you have an entire harem of women to select from. What do you want with me?"

He didn't like the way that made him sound, like a womanizer governed only by self-gratification. That wasn't him. "Who told you that?"

She noted that he wasn't denying it. "I've been coming here for over a week now. I hear the nurses talking." Amusement rose to her eyes. "It's amazing, given the social life you're reported to have, that you have time to fit in any doctoring."

Being a doctor had never taken second place in his life. "Number one, people exaggerate, you know that. Number two, I haven't been out with anyone since I pulled you and your grandfather out of the car." And he hadn't. He and Diana had never gotten together for that evening he'd canceled and he had absolutely no desire to pick up where he'd left off.

Vienna had taken center stage and there were no understudies.

God help her, she believed him. "Is that because we had a moment?" Vienna asked wryly.

"I'm not sure what we had," he told her honestly. "But we had something. I just want to find out what that something is. And I thought that dinner might be a good place to start." And then he did smile. "Besides, I think it might make your grandfather happy."

Her grandfather was the kind of man who could take an inch, stretch it out and build a freeway on it. He'd done it before. "What would make my grandfather happy is if I was married with six kids."

Not so unusual, Georges thought. And her saying this didn't make him want to run for the hills. The thought of running didn't enter his mind.

"Every journey starts with the first step," he told her, then put his hand out to hers. He sensed he had an advantage and he pressed it. "How about it? Tonight? At seven?"

Vienna regarded the hand, but held back from taking it. "And I get to pick the place?"

"Absolutely."

"The cafeteria."

His eyes narrowed as he tried to follow her. "What cafeteria?"

As if it were a done deal, she placed her hand in

his, sealing a bargain he hadn't yet agreed to. "The one in the basement."

"You want to eat in the hospital cafeteria." He repeated the words, too stunned by the choice even to form them into a question.

Her eyes shone as she nodded. There were reasons for her choice. She told him the most obvious one. "This way, if anything comes up with my grandfather, you won't be far away and neither will I."

Georges was fairly confident that nothing would come up. Yesterday's code blue had been an aberration. All of Amos's vitals looked good today. "You know, I can afford better than the cafeteria."

"I'm sure you can," she replied. "But I sampled some of the cafeteria food from my grandfather's tray the other day. It's not bad."

There was a challenge in her voice. If he tried to argue her out of her choice, he had a feeling she'd change her mind and decline the invitation altogether.

Better than nothing, Georges told himself. "If that's what it takes to have dinner with you, then the cafeteria it is."

He could have sworn that the smile on her face was a wee bit nervous around the edges.

His day over, Georges changed and then made his way over to Amos's room. He was early and

Vienna wasn't waiting outside the room, or inside it once he walked in.

Since he was there, he decided to recheck the old man's vitals one more time. Nurses came by to do a periodic update, but he had never liked being idle.

Greeting the man, Georges began to take his pulse.

Amos eyed him closely. "I hear you're taking my Vienna out for dinner."

He nodded, releasing the man's wrist. "Just to the cafeteria."

"The cafeteria?" Amos repeated incredulously. The old man looked at him as if he'd lost his mind. "This cafeteria? The one in the hospital?"

Georges laughed and nodded. "Afraid so."

Amos hit the controls on his handrail, raising the back of his bed a little more. He stared at the younger man, confused. "Listen, boy, if it is a matter of money, I can—"

Georges stopped him before the man could make an offer and embarrass him. "Thank you for the thought but it's your granddaughter's choice. She wants both of us to be close by in case you need us."

Amos opened his mouth to protest, then closed it again. And then he smiled. Broadly. "She is one in a million, that girl." Amos looked at Georges, his blue-gray eyes all the more imposing beneath tufts of gray eyebrows. "You do know that, do you not?"

She was certainly different, Georges thought,

he'd give her that. He couldn't think of a single woman he'd ever been with who would have been satisfied with being taken to a cafeteria. "I am beginning to get that impression."

Amos looked at him for a long moment, as if debating saying what he was about to tell him. And then he made up his mind. The man needed to know just how unique Vienna was. "Not everyone breaks up with their fiancé because they put family first."

The information caught Georges off guard. And made him feel oddly hollow. "She's engaged?"

"Was," Amos corrected firmly. "Six months ago. Before we moved here from New York." He didn't know how much Vienna had told the young physician. Probably not much, if he knew Vienna. She was friendly and outgoing, but closemouthed at the same time. Not an easy feat. "My doctor said I needed to come out here for my health, get away from the cold, wet winters before they got the better of me," he explained. For a moment, he closed his eyes. "It meant starting over again at my age."

Georges had no doubt that the man had probably been up to it, but still, it seemed like a lonely proposition if he had to do it by himself.

"Vienna would not hear of me coming out alone. She wanted us to move as a family. Me, her and Edward." By the way he said the name, Georges had the feeling that Amos was not too keen on Edward. "Edward refused and told her it was about time she grew up and made an adult choice." He fairly beamed. "So she did." And then his smile receded as he clearly relived the scenario. "I did not want to stand in the way of her happiness and told her I would be fine, but she wouldn't listen. Said that since I did not ask her to choose, she picked me."

He leaned in closer to Georges. "To tell you the truth, I am glad. Not because I love her company or because she has a wonderful business head on her shoulders, but because that Edward was not any good for her. He did not appreciate the girl that she was."

"Doesn't sound like he did," Georges agreed. It earned him a wide, approving smile from Amos.

"Everything was always about him, never about her," Amos continued. "You can not love someone if you do not put them first." He looked at Georges for a long moment, as if to see if his words had penetrated. "Do you understand what I am saying?"

Lessons in love from a seventy-four-year-old, Georges mused. He did his best not to grin. "I do."

"Good," Amos pronounced. He was about to say more, but the door to his room opened. Wearing a simple blue sheath and her hair pinned back from her face, Vienna entered.

She looked suspiciously from one to the other. "What are you to talking about?" she asked.

"I was just telling him to let an old man rest," Amos informed her, never missing a beat. He waved a thin hand toward the door, then closed his eyes. "I am tired."

She crossed to the bed. "Don't you even say hello?" she asked him.

He opened one eye for a moment. "Hello. Goodbye." His eyes were shut again.

With a laugh, she leaned over and brushed her lips against his cheek. "Good night, you old devil."

She thought she heard him chuckle as she left the room with Georges.

The elevator was crowded. Georges and Vienna made their way to the rear, claiming a space as best they could. She stood in front of him. He was aware of the scent of her hair, aware of her body as it pressed against his.

Georges lowered his head so that she could hear him. "Not too late to change your mind about eating here," he told her as the elevator made a stop on the second floor. "I hear I can still get a table at McDonald's without having to book it first."

She turned slightly, brushing her hair against his lowered face. "The cafeteria is fine," she told him. "I have very simple tastes, Doctor." They stopped at the first floor and most of the elevator emptied. Taking advantage of the space, she took a step to the side and turned to look at him. "This isn't about the food, anyway."

The scent he'd detected earlier seemed stronger somehow, wrapping itself all around him. "What is it about?"

"Getting to know each other." Her eyes searched his face to see if he agreed. "That's why people go out, isn't it?"

It would have been simple to coast and go along with everything she said. But something about her demanded the truth from him at all times. "Sometimes."

"And other times?" The elevator doors opened in the basement and they stepped off, along with a nurse and another person.

He took her arm. "And other times, it's just a prelude to the real point of the evening."

They made their way down the winding corridor to the cafeteria doors. Subdued noise greeted them as they entered. She turned toward him. "Which is?"

He laughed shortly, shaking his head. Maybe he should have just agreed after all. "You don't make this easy, do you?"

She stopped short of entering the food service area. "It can be as easy or as hard as you like, Doctor. But I really do value honesty."

He plunged ahead before he could weigh his options. "All right, here's some honesty for you.

You've been on my mind since I first pulled you out of the car. For some reason, I can't stop thinking about you and that's saying a lot since, as you seem to know already, I don't exactly live like a monk.

"I postponed a date to remain with you," he continued, drawing her aside as another couple made their way into the cafeteria, "which isn't unusual. But then I didn't reschedule, which is." The more serious he became, the lower his voice grew. "I haven't wanted to see anyone else since I met you, which is *definitely* unusual for me. You kissed me that first evening and ever since I keep wondering what it would be like to make love to you. I think about it almost all the time, even when I don't want to be. I have to admit that I'm not really happy about it because I never wanted to commit to anything but my work—and now…I don't know anymore."

For a very long moment after he finished, she said nothing. She wasn't exactly sure what she'd expected him to say, but this was far more than she'd been prepared for. He'd overwhelmed her. Overwhelmed her and taken her breath away.

It took her a moment to find it. And to make up her mind.

Vienna smiled up at him. "You weren't kidding about being honest, were you?"

"No, and I'm not kidding about anything else, either," he told her.

"All right." Slowly, she nodded her head, her eyes never leaving his. "All right," she repeated, turning away from the food service area.

He'd blown it, Georges thought. A feeling of desperation, of wanting to fix what had been broken, washed over him. But he hadn't a clue where to start. He could only ask numbly, "All right what?"

She touched his face before answering, her fingertips lightly gliding along his skin. Her heart hammering wildly in her chest. "All right, we'll go to my place. So you can stop wondering what it would be like to make love with me."

Chapter Ten

It took Georges several seconds to regain use of his tongue, which, along with the rest of him, had momentarily gone numb after Vienna's invitation. He stared at her now, wondering if he'd misheard. "You're kidding."

Nerves shimmied up her spine, but she'd come too far to back down. "I never kid about something like that."

Georges continued looking at her, somewhat uncertain. It wasn't like him to refuse an offer like this from someone he was interested in. But the offer itself confused him. Perhaps for the first time in his life, he felt like a man standing on the middle of a tightrope without a clue about how he'd gotten there.

He wanted to make sure he hadn't misunderstood. "You're sure?"

She sighed and laughed at the same time, confusion reigning supreme. "God, no."

The laugh was a nervous one. The mystery deepened. Was he missing something? "Then why…?"

She took a breath. "Because I know it just has to be."

"Another 'feeling?'"

For lack of a better way to explain it, she agreed. "Something like that."

But her feeling had nothing to do with touching him and that ensuing sensation that sometimes carried a premonition. There was no premonition here. She just had a need, an overwhelming, stunning need she couldn't ignore, even though this would probably turn out badly for her.

And yet, she couldn't make herself walk away. Couldn't make herself run and hide, to wait this out. Because if not tonight, then tomorrow, or the day after that, when she least expected it, she'd succumb. She'd wind up making love with him. This way, while her grandfather was still in the hospital for one more day, she could call the shots.

Sort of.

Okay, he thought, this was good. This was better than good. Working hard to keep his brain from scrambling, he tried to remember his manners. "Do you want to have something to eat first?"

She pressed her lips together. Committed, she needed to see this through. "No."

He'd assumed that she'd suggested the cafeteria because the noise and people were, in a way, a protective shield for her. To keep their relationship from moving forward. Now that they were all but racing to the finish line, there was no more need for that kind of barrier. "I mean in a really decent restaurant."

Vienna didn't say anything. Instead, she gazed at him for a long moment. The longing she felt inside, the hunger eating away at her, grew to almost unbearable proportions.

Maybe it was because of everything she'd been through these last few days. Maybe it was fueled by the emotional turmoil she'd endured, confronted with her grandfather's mortality.

Or maybe it just had to do with the extremely magnetic connection she felt whenever she was around this larger-than-life heroic doctor. She didn't know. All she knew was that *this* really needed to happen between them. "No."

Well, he'd tried, Georges thought. And to be honest, eating was the furthest thing from his mind right now. Calmly breaking bread in a five-star restaurant might be more than he could manage to pull off at the moment.

"All right, then," he agreed. "Your place."

Her eyes held his for a flickering of eternity. "My place," she repeated.

Vienna's hand was trembling as she tried to put the large silver key into her front door lock. Trembling so hard that her first attempt to open the door failed. The key ring slipped from her hand and fell with a jarring clang to the blue-and-gray welcome mat.

Before she could pick them up again, Georges stooped down beside her and retrieved the keys. He selected the right key and unlocked the door for her.

But even as he placed his hand on the doorknob, he refrained from turning it. Instead, he whispered to her, "You don't have to do this, you know. We can just turn around and—"

Placing her hand over his, Vienna pushed down and opened the door. She entered her house and swung around in the foyer in one smooth motion.

The next moment, her mouth was sealed against his lips.

Sealed as closely as her body was to his, filling every space between them until there wasn't enough left for a whisper of air.

Something suddenly ignited between them. Within them.

It occurred so fast that whatever breath Georges thought he had left was stolen away. He'd never had that happen with a woman before. Oh, he'd been breathless before, but always by his own design and calculation. And he had always, always been in control of the situation, of the moment.

Here, he was free-falling without a single recollection of how it had begun.

Only that it was.

He liked to make love to a woman at his own pace, but with Vienna, he was losing control. There was an urgency that spurred him on, running like a flame along fuel that had been spilled on the ground, speeding to encompass every inch.

Within moments of slamming shut the door, holding Vienna's supple form trapped between the wall and his body, Georges swiftly stripped her. She did the same for him. Shirt, pants, dress and assorted undergarments went flying in all directions, a flurry of material and colors left to fend for themselves.

Georges wanted her with a fierceness that made his teeth ache. It would have scared the hell out of him if he'd taken so much as a microsecond to pause and consider. But he couldn't. All he could do was hold on for dear life.

Hold on and savor.

God, could he savor, he thought, his lips traveling up and down the length of her throat, the breadth of her breasts. Thoughts and desires all swirled into one another as he methodically worked his way down her torso.

Then, dropping to his knees, he continued to hold her against the wall as best he could while moving downward, ever downward.

He heard her whimper and thought he would dissolve in a cloud of vapor.

Small, almost animal-like noises escaped from her lips. His tongue caressed her in all the places that his hands, his mouth, touched. Her whole body felt as if it were vibrating. Throbbing.

She could hardly breathe as she wound her fingers through his hair, pressing him against her. Urging him not to stop even as her body jerked and trembled. The sensation that exploded within her as his tongue found her inner core caused the world to go dark just for a heartbeat. Weakened, she all but sagged down to her knees beside him.

But then he pushed her back, weaving the magic more forcefully, more urgently this time until another climax found her. Rocked her. Sounds, almost guttural, rose in her throat, lodging there, fighting for space with her ragged breath.

With her last bit of strength, her fingers digging into his shoulders, Vienna managed to drag him back up to her level.

Or maybe he came of his own volition, she wasn't sure. All she knew was that the next moment, he was kissing her and their bodies were entwined.

She could feel him harden against her. Jumping up, she wrapped her legs around his torso, her invitation clear. With a sob, she cried out his name as Georges drove himself into her.

Her head spun.

She began to move against him, more and more urgently. His arms tightening around her so hard she could hardly breathe. All the while, their lips slanted over and over again in kiss after endless kiss. They reached the apex together. She thought his lips would be forever imprinted upon hers.

And then, suddenly, they were tumbling onto her sofa, their bodies covered in a slick sheen of sweat as exhaustion drenched them both. His back was to the cushions and she was on top of him and far too spent to notice.

She was never going to draw a normal breath again, Vienna thought as her chest continued to heave. But that was all right, she told herself, because her head was lost in the stars.

As was the rest of her.

After what seemed like an eternity, Georges opened his eyes and looked up at her. "You are a surprise, Vienna Hollenbeck," he marveled fondly.

Vienna felt a smile spreading in response.

"You're not." She took a moment to draw more air into her lungs. Would there ever be enough again? "You're exactly what I thought you'd be."

Well, that made one of them, he thought. Because he'd even surprised himself with the level of sensations that had telegraphed through him. With the desire that had all but torn him in half as it rammed itself into his body. As for his level of exhaustion, well, even at his most vigorous, he'd never felt as if he'd just run a twenty-six-mile marathon.

Shifting, he continued to hold her against him, feeling her warmth seeping into his body. Arousing him. Was that possible at this point? If he was half-dead, did that mean he was half-alive?

He felt her smile against his side. Georges raised an eyebrow as he looked into her face.

"Is this cuddling?" There was amusement in her voice. Had that ex-fiancé never held her as if she were something precious? While the thought took form, he felt the sting of something unpleasant.

Jealousy?

"This is called holding on for dear life until the room stops spinning," he informed her whimsically, using humor to hide the fact that his own reactions had left him shaken.

Vienna dug herself out of the pocket he'd created for her. Propping herself up on her elbow, she looked down at him. The tips of her blond hair skimmed lightly, teasingly, over his chest with each word she spoke.

He began to feel his stomach tightening in anticipation.

"Does this mean that you don't want to do it again?" she asked.

More than he wanted to breathe, he thought. But there were limitations.

"There's a world of difference between desire and execution," Georges told her. "I'm afraid that you're going to have to give me a few minutes so I can pull myself together."

Hand planted on his chest, she pushed him back against the cushions. Leaning over his face, her lips grazed his so lightly it was almost more of a promise of a kiss than an actual kiss.

"How few?" she whispered, her breath caressing his skin. Smiling, she glided just the very tip of her tongue along the outline of his mouth, moving back out of reach when he tried to kiss her. There was laughter in her eyes.

He could feel his blood quickening, could feel the adrenaline surging as the anticipation of another wild ride began to form.

Craning his neck up away from the sofa cushion, Georges cupped her face between his hands and brought it down so that his mouth captured hers. He kissed her long and hard as all systems came back on line, declaring their readiness to go at will.

"This few," he said against her mouth before he kissed her again.

They went slower this time, but still fast enough to all but set the sofa cushions on fire.

Their positions were reversed. While she had been the one to take the initiative before, only to have him steal the reins from her, this time around Georges began their intimate dance only to have her suddenly take over the lead.

Vienna feasted on his body just the way he had on hers earlier, driving him crazy with desire until he was fairly certain he would have given her anything she asked for.

He knew he'd willingly given her his soul.

They made love twice more until, both spent beyond all reason or measure, Georges and Vienna fell asleep in each other's arms.

Georges slowly stirred. It took him a moment to realize that his eyes were shut. He'd fallen asleep. The same moment that occurred to him, what had preceded came back to him in vivid color.

Vienna, lighting his world the way it had never been lit before.

Vienna.

The emptiness beside him registered even before

he opened his eyes. As did an incredible feeling of abandonment. That was something he'd never felt before. Something he was quick to bank down. Because it was so unlike him, he attributed it to the strange way the evening had unfolded.

"Vienna?"

There was no answer. He scrubbed his hand over his face, trying to pull himself together. Trying to get his brain back in focus.

Light came in from the hallway. It was still dark outside. That meant not too much time had lapsed. How much was not too much? He couldn't make out the numbers on his wrist watch.

Getting up, Georges quickly pulled on his pants. For the time being, he left everything else off. He needed to find out where Vienna was before he thought about mundane things like socks.

The moment he left the bedroom, he heard noise coming from below. Someone was up and about downstairs. He padded down the stairs, his bare feet brushing against the raised design of the gray carpeting.

Rather than call out her name again, he decided to silently investigate her whereabouts.

To his relief and somewhat surprise, he found Vienna in the kitchen. Her back to the entrance, she was wearing a coverall apron that draped loosely over a pair of jeans and a blue pullover sweater.

He would have preferred seeing her in just the apron alone.

As he crossed the threshold, he saw that Vienna had slipped something into the microwave oven. She pressed a combination of buttons on the keypad, then Start. The light went on inside the microwave and the turntable rotated.

Georges snuck up behind her, then slipped his arms around her waist, pulling her against his chest. She didn't squeal in surprise.

He had a feeling she'd probably seen his reflection in the shiny surface of the toaster that stood next to the microwave. "I thought you weren't hungry."

She placed her hands over his, not to remove them but, for the moment, to press them even more tightly against her. Absorbing his strength.

"I didn't say that." And then she turned in the circle of his arms until she faced him and could look up into his eyes. "I was just more hungry for something else."

Before Georges could teasingly make reference to her other appetite, she rose on her toes and brushed her lips against his. Once, twice and then a third time, each pass lasting a little bit longer than the last. And then, wrapping her arms around his neck, Vienna kissed him long and hard.

She was smiling when she finally drew her head back to look at him again.

"What?" he asked.

Her smile was positively wicked as her eyes dipped down to just below his waist. "It feels as if you want to play again."

He laughed, holding her closer again. She made him feel carefree and yet serious at the same time. "Is that what you call it now? 'Playing?'"

Vienna nodded her head. Playing. That was the label she had to put on it. Because, she sensed, calling it anything more serious might scare him off. Georges was not a man who played for keeps, he was a man who merely played.

And she, well, she wasn't altogether sure what she was right now. A little while ago, she would have said that when she played, it was for all the marbles. Because making love with someone was very serious to her. But being with Georges even this one time had changed all the rules on her. It didn't, ultimately, make her want any less, but it made her willing to settle for less.

Because wanting more, asking for more, would only give her nothing. She was going to have to take this man on his terms—drawing them out a little more each time, until perhaps, just perhaps, his terms and hers met somewhere in the middle. Until then—if *then* ever came—she was more than willing to dance this strange dance whose music she found filling her head.

"Uh-huh," she murmured just before he deepened the kiss she had initiated.

And then, as he came up for air, Georges grinned as he looked into her eyes. "You've got my head spinning so much, I could swear I hear bells ringing."

"You did," she told him, her mouth curving. When he looked at her, puzzled, she explained, "That's the microwave." Vienna nodded her head toward the counter. "I think it's done."

"But I'm not," he told her just before he lowered his mouth to hers again.

Chapter Eleven

Amos Schwarzwalden gripped the arms of his wheelchair, not for support but because he couldn't wait to be free of it. He'd insisted that he could walk across the hospital threshold to his freedom, but Shelly, the cute day nurse he'd been flirting with for the last few days, had informed him that use of the wheelchair was mandatory hospital policy. No one was released from an overnight stay at Blair Memorial unless they were wheeled out.

He'd promised not to sue, no matter what happened, but the nurse just continued to look at him until he finally got off the bed and reluctantly lowered himself into the wheelchair.

Watching the exchange, both verbal and silent, Vienna gave serious thought to kidnapping the young woman and bringing her home with them. Shelly seemed to be able to handle her grandfather a lot better than she could.

Much to Amos's obvious dismay, Shelly was not the one taking him down to the front entrance. But he lit up again when he saw who was.

Georges.

That made two of them, Vienna thought, returning the greeting the doctor tendered to first her grandfather, then to her. Was it her imagination, or had his eyes lingered on her a little longer?

At times like this, it was hard to remember that she was a grown woman with one lengthy relationship, not to mention engagement, behind her. Especially when her pulse insisted on racing.

"You are taking me out of here?" Amos asked, craning his neck to look at Georges more closely.

Georges took hold of the wheelchair's handles. "I insisted." He glanced again in Vienna's direction. "Ready?"

"I am," Amos declared, as exuberant as a schoolboy about to embark on his first day of summer vacation.

Georges began to push the chair out of the room and down the hallway. "Then we're on our way."

Vienna fell into place beside him. She wore that perfume of hers again, he noted. The one that instantly drugged him and brought intimate images into his mind. It filled the empty service elevator just enough so that he couldn't concentrate. Amos was talking to him and he hadn't heard a single word.

"Do not be a stranger, now," Amos said as they left the confines of the elevator car. Georges took a deep breath, trying to counteract the effects of Vienna's sensual scent. "Remember, I want you to feel free to come by the bakery at any time." They took the shortest route to the front entrance, making their way down a newly recarpeted corridor. "There will always be a box of pastries waiting for you." Turning again in his seat, this time to the other side, Amos glanced slyly at his granddaughter. "Among other things perhaps."

She'd been pushy enough for both of them last night, Vienna thought. Georges didn't need her grandfather applying pressure, as well. The man was as subtle as a cave-in.

"Grandpa," she admonished, "Dr. Armand has more important things to do than spend his free time hanging around Vienna's Finest."

Amos was not easily daunted. "Every man needs to relax a little."

Vienna laughed shortly. "This from a man who refuses to even lie down when he's sick."

"I am not sick," Amos insisted with feeling. "I am healthy, right, Georges?" He turned his head toward the younger man for backup. "Otherwise, they would not be letting me go from this fine establishment." He waited for agreement. "Am I correct?"

"Absolutely," Georges told him, doing his best to look somber. Satisfied, Amos turned back around to face front. Georges caught the concerned look in Vienna's eye. "Just remember not to overdo it," Georges warned.

Amos nodded his head. "I will remember."

A small "Ha!" escaped Vienna's lips. When he looked at her, she pointed out, "Notice that my grandfather promised that he'd remember, not that he wouldn't overdo it." Her grandfather was well versed when it came to artfully dodging any appeals regarding taking life a little easier.

Amos sighed, clasping his hands in his lap. "I have you for that."

"You'd better believe it," Vienna assured him with feeling. She intended to be his nurse and his keeper until she was satisfied that he had fully recovered.

Georges pushed the wheelchair across the threshold as the electronic doors drew open for them. The late-morning air was welcoming and sultry. Just like Vienna, he caught himself thinking. Georges brought the wheelchair to a stop on the wide rubber welcome mat just beyond the threshold.

Amos shifted so that he could see him. His smile was warm, appealing. Another trait he shared with his granddaughter, Georges thought.

"Well, my young friend, I cannot say it has not been interesting." Leaning forward, he took Georges' hand and instead of shaking it, held it in both of his. Despite the various conditions that had stricken him, he was still a short bull of a man with powerful hands. "And I am very glad that you have come into our lives, mine and Vienna's. Very glad," he underscored, still clasping the doctor's hand. He beamed. "I will see you again."

"Count on it. I want to see you back here for a checkup with Dr. Schulman in two weeks." He raised his eyes to Vienna's face for a confirmation. She nodded, but it was Amos who answered. His tone was less than glowing when he spoke of the surgeon.

"Ah, yes, Dr. Schulman. The man who does not smile." Amos shook his head, as if he pitied anyone who found life so somber. Vienna had mentioned that her grandfather had been a boy in Austria during World War II and had endured a great many hardships, only some of which he shared with her. That the man found the will and the strength only to look at the bright side of life was an amazing testimonial to his character. "I will see him, too. But you, you are the one I *want* to see."

Georges nodded and slowly extricated his hand. For a moment, he made no comment. Instead, he looked over toward Vienna. He'd left her house in the wee hours of the morning instead of staying the night. He'd wanted to, God help him, but it was something, as a rule, he never did.

Looking at her, he felt regret rippling through him, surfacing out of the shadows. A first, he thought as he felt a warmth spread over him because he was looking at her. Nothing more.

Another first. He was going to have to get hold of himself, he silently promised.

But for now, there were last-minute instructions to give. "A home health care nurse will be calling you this afternoon," he told both of them "I've seen to the paperwork myself." And he had, calling in a favor so that Amos would be given the maximum amount of care for a minimum cost. He'd promised to take care of the rest, making sure no one told either the old man or Vienna.

"Make sure she's young," Amos requested with a wicked wink. "And pretty."

"Make sure she's fast," Vienna added. She smiled fondly down at her grandfather. "He's pretty quick when he wants to be."

"I'll pass that along," Georges said, then asked, "Can I speak to you for a moment?"

"Sure."

Securing Amos's wheelchair so that it wouldn't roll away, Georges stepped over to the side. Vienna followed, then waited, holding her breath. Afraid that he was going to say something he didn't want her grandfather to hear, something about Amos's health that he hadn't been apprised of.

"Yes?" she pressed when he didn't say anything immediately.

Georges took in a subtle breath. "I'd like to see you again. Once your grandfather's settled in and there's a routine in place," he added quickly. Damn it, he was tripping over his tongue. When was the last time that that had happened? To his recollection, never. It was her doing, all hers.

Run, an urgent voice in his head ordered. *Run now, while you still can.*

It *was* something he didn't want her grandfather to hear, Vienna thought, a smile blossoming on her lips. But an entirely different something than she'd initially thought. A lovely something. She was so relieved, she could have cried.

"I'd like that," she answered softly. "Why don't you take him up on his invitation? Come by the house, say tomorrow night for dinner?"

Georges could see that Amos was trying very

hard to hear what they were saying and still appear not to be listening. He found it hard not to smile. "His invitation was for the bakery," he reminded her.

"Bakery, house, there's not much difference. My grandfather practically lives at the bakery and I'm sure he will again, once he's well."

He liked the idea of seeing her again. And the idea of having a chaperon might help keep things in check until he figured out just what was going on here. "What time?" he asked.

That was purely up to him, she thought. "When can you make it?"

For a second, Georges tried to remember his schedule. Most of the time, it was up in the air. His shift could get switched around at any time, entirely at the discretion of the attending physician or anyone else who outranked him.

"I'm going to have to get back to you on that later today," he confessed.

She began to reach into her purse. "You need my cell number?"

He put his hand on hers, stopping her. Or maybe it was his smile that did it. She couldn't think when her bones were melting faster than snow in July. "Still have it from when you gave it to me at the hospital the first time."

"Okay. Good." She nodded, pleased more than she could possibly say. Her grandfather was coming home and Georges had just indicated that last night wasn't just a glorious one-night stand but perhaps something with a little more substance. God was in His heaven and all was right with the world. "Can you wait with my grandfather while I bring up the car?" She caught her lower lip between her teeth as she waited for his answer.

Georges felt his gut tighten. He wanted to kiss her. But he was good at keeping his true thoughts from showing on his face. So he nodded and gave her the easy smile that everyone always associated with him.

"My pleasure," he told her.

"Thank you. Be right back." Vienna hurried across a crosswalk out to the aboveground parking lot located on the far side of the hospital grounds.

"Wonderful girl," Amos commented as his granddaughter disappeared from view. He turned to see if Georges was watching her.

Not so much a girl as a woman, Georges thought. A woman who'd managed to set his world on its ear. "That she is."

"Do not know what I would do without her." And the old man meant that from the bottom of his soul. It seemed ironic to him that somewhere along the line, the tables had gotten turned and the little girl he'd taken care of was now taking care of him. "But I would give her up to the right man," Amos told him, still craning his neck so that he could study the face of the man standing behind him.

Meaning me? Georges couldn't help wondering what the old man would say if he knew about his reputation.

At this point, he honestly didn't know if he should follow his needs or go with his instincts. The latter told him to stop this before it got out of hand. Before he lost his heart to this woman and suffered the consequences.

Before, that same voice mocked. Too late for that.

Was this what his mother felt? Fear? Fear of being out on that limb, only to find himself abandoned.

His mother left lovers before they could leave her. Years ago, he'd realized that it was because she was afraid of giving her heart to someone who would either abuse her love or break her heart in two. Despite all her fame, Lily Moreau had been through a great deal.

He and his brothers generally agreed that Philippe's father had been the love of her life, but he'd also been a hopeless gambler, far more enamored of Lady Luck than he was of Lily. He all but gambled away the very roof over their heads. Had she not taken drastic measures to save them, he would have. After that, she never put her faith or trust into one man, although she'd been twice tempted, with his own father and with Alain's. But both marriages were tempestuous and relatively short-lived. No man was a match, it seemed, for the dynamic and larger-than-life Lily Moreau.

Because there was no stability for him to use as a compass, Georges had picked his way through life much the way his mother had, enjoying the company of the opposite sex and then, when the threat of something more serious was in the offing, he would move on. Life had been free and easy with no strings, no pain hiding in the shadows, waiting to seize him when he least expected it.

And there was no lasting love hiding to capture him, either.

Lasting love. Was there such a thing? he wondered as he stood there, watching Vienna pull up to the curb in her vehicle. At this point, he didn't know.

"Okay, your chariot awaits, Grandpa," she announced, swinging her legs out of the driver's side.

Vienna came around the back of the vehicle to help him out of the wheelchair. From what she had seen, he was still a little wobbly on his legs and she didn't want to risk having him hurt himself.

Between her and Georges, they managed to successfully lower Amos into the passenger side of the front seat. Georges drew away the wheelchair, locking the wheels so that it wouldn't suddenly go rolling down the winding path. With that out of the way, he closed Amos's door. Vienna rounded the front of the vehicle and he looked at her over the roof.

"I'll call you," he repeated.

Something in Georges' voice, a vague distance she hadn't heard before, planted a seed of doubt in her head. Worse, in her heart. But she told herself she was just imagining things. So she smiled at him and nodded.

"Until then," she replied warmly. Secretly hoping that was enough to make him want to keep his word.

"Don't you look at your messages?" Georges heard Philippe's voice in his ear as he answered his cell phone more than a week later. There was suppressed irritation in his brother's tone, simmering just beneath the surface.

Georges was feeling too good to get defensive. Life had been hectic, but progressing rather well these days. As promised, he'd secured the nurse for Amos and it had turned out to be a perfect match. The old man still hadn't gotten to the point where he could go back to the bakery for anything but a short visit, but he was progressing well.

Things were progressing well between him and Vienna, too, he thought. So well that he caught himself waiting for a mythical shoe to drop.

Or maybe the bottom to fall out.

But most of the time, he refused to allow himself to think about it beyond the moment. There was safety in ignorance, he thought.

Georges knew what his brother was referring to. Not messages left on his cell phone, but on his computer. Philippe had made his money and a name for himself developing software for large companies. He lived and breathed the computer.

The same was not true of him.

"E-mail is not something I usually have time for," Georges told him. "I don't know about you, but I'm still connected to the rest of the world by phone. Now, what is it I was supposed to have read and, I'm guessing, responded to?"

"Mother's having a show tomorrow. She wants all of us to be there."

By all, he knew Philippe was referring to not just him and his other brother, but Philippe's fiancée and Janice's daughter, Kelli, a five-year-old Lily doted on. Gordon, Janice's brother, had gotten pulled into the circle, as well, plus assorted cousins. Alain usually brought his date of the moment with him. He, on the other hand, never did.

He was outside of Blair, taking one of his rare breaks. Georges leaned against the wall, the cell phone to his ear. "You know, when we were kids, all her shows were usually located halfway around the country. We practically had to make appointments to see her. Now she's here much more than she's not. Why the change?" he asked.

Philippe, as always, had all the answers. He laughed softly. "Age."

"Mother doesn't age," Georges reminded him. Other people's mothers aged. Lily Moreau had her portrait hidden somewhere in someone's attic. *It* was aging while she did not.

"She wishes," Philippe said with a laugh. "No, I'm serious. I think somewhere along the line, it finally hit her that she'd missed out on a lot on the home front, flying around the way she did while we were growing up on her. Probably, in her mind, she's trying to make up for lost time."

Georges had another theory about what could've brought about this change in their mother. She'd always been a loving mother in her own way, but she'd never stayed in their lives for such a long stretch of time before. "I think it's you getting married that probably triggered all this."

There was silence on the other end as Philippe considered his words. "Maybe," he allowed. "At any rate, no matter what brought this on, bottom line is she wants us to show up."

Georges hesitated. He was on duty in the evening for the rest of the week. "I can't unless I find someone to trade hours with—"

Philippe laughed. Their mother was way ahead

of him on that. "The chief of surgery at Blair's a friend of Mother's. She's already made sure you have the evening off."

Typical, Georges thought. She might have seemed like a hurricane blowing into town, but Lily always liked being in control, always liked calling the shots. "Why couldn't we have had the kind of mother who liked to put on an apron and bake cookies?"

"Because then she wouldn't have been Lily Moreau—and for all we know, if she followed that kind of lifestyle, you and Alain might have never been born. She would have stuck by my father through thick and thin."

Philippe had a point. In any case, they'd never know. "So, what's so special about this showing? She just had one a few months ago."

"This one's for Kyle. They're his paintings."

Kyle, their mother's so-called latest "companion." Now that he thought of it, Georges remembered her saying something about Kyle having a great deal of potential. So, she was talking about his ability to paint, not something else. But could he paint well enough for a show? "The boy toy?"

"One and the same, except I think Mother sees him as something more than that."

Georges suppressed a groan. While "Lily in love" was more like a force of nature, he didn't exactly relish this particular choice she'd made. "She's had countless 'companions' since Alain's father died. What makes you think that this guy in short pants is so important to her?"

There was another pregnant pause on the other end, longer this time, as if Philippe were composing his thoughts. "You haven't noticed the resemblance?"

Georges had no idea what he was talking about. "To who?"

"To my father."

For a second, Georges was speechless. Until Philippe had said it, there had only been that vague recognition echoing in the recesses of his mind, the kind that haunted people when they saw someone they thought they knew, but weren't sure.

"Oh God, you're right."

Philippe's father was the only one of their mother's partners and lovers with whom she ever reunited on an intimate basis. After she divorced his own father, she took Philippe's back for a while, although they didn't get married the second time around. But the reunion was short-lived. The final straw came when she discovered that his gambling affliction was worse than ever.

Despite the turbulent nature of their last breakup, she was inconsolable when she discovered that the man had died, taken by a brain aneurysm that had suddenly ruptured.

"Do you think that's why she's with him?" Georges asked.

"That's part of it. The other part is that our eternally young mother wants to remain that way. I think that Kyle is her second chance at being twenty-five again."

A thought suddenly pushed its way forward, stealing Georges' breath away. "You don't think she's going to wind up marrying him, do you?"

"Hard to say. This is Mother we're talking about, a woman who has never played by any rules known to the ordinary man."

Philippe was right. Of all of them, he was the one who knew her best. "What do you think of him?"

"He's young."

"Other than that," Georges said impatiently. He got to the heart of the matter. "Do you think that he's after her money?"

"Personally, I think he's as dazzled by her as the rest of the world is. She needs that right now, needs to be the center of someone's universe."

"She could have been that by being more of a mother and less of a celebrity when we were growing up."

"Can't change the past," Philippe told him. "Can only work with the present and the future." He had to get going, and he still didn't have the answer he wanted. The least emotional of her three sons, he was still very protective of his part-time mother. "So, are you coming?"

It sounded as if his showing up was important to Philippe. "Are you asking?"

"I'm asking."

He owed Philippe more than he could ever possibly repay. "Then I'm coming." He hesitated for a moment, debating asking, then decided he had nothing to lose. "If I bring someone with me, do you think that'll cause any ripples?"

"Are you bringing that woman you've been seeing?"

Georges picked up the inference in his brother's tone. Defensive instincts kicked in. "I never mentioned a specific woman."

"You didn't have to. Do I think it'll cause ripples? Probably. But as long as it's not a tsunami, you'll survive. Bring her. I think I'd like to meet the woman who finally nailed my brother's hide to the wall."

Georges anticipated the repercussions. He changed his mind. "Forget it. I'm coming alone."

Philippe's laugh said that he knew better, but for now, he'd play along. "Suit yourself. See you at the gallery tomorrow night."

Chapter Twelve

Georges smiled to himself as he closed his cell phone and put it back into his pocket. Good old Philippe. His brother always knew that the fastest way to get him to do something was to tell him not to. That much about their relationship hadn't changed.

While the inclination was still fresh, he'd placed a call to Vienna and caught her at home instead of the bakery. She was having lunch with her grandfather. He kept the conversation short and asked her if she wanted to come with him to the show at the gallery.

The words were barely out of his mouth before

she eagerly accepted the invitation he'd tendered. It was only after he'd terminated the connection that he began to wonder what he was letting himself in for and why he was doing it in the first place.

No quick answers came to mind. And those that did he wasn't up to contemplating.

Tomorrow night was going to be one hell of an interesting evening.

"Are you sure you're going to be all right, Grandpa?" It was the third time in as many minutes that she asked the question.

Vienna was dressed in a shimmering electric-blue cocktail dress that flirted with the middle of her thighs. Georges was close to mesmerized by the way the hem moved and swayed along her skin. She'd been ready to leave now for more than ten minutes, yet couldn't quite get herself to go.

No premonition kept her from leaving with Georges, who looked so dashing tonight in his black tux. It was just that her grandfather's color was so pale, she was afraid something would happen to him while she was away.

"Better question is will Silvia be all right?" Amos replied, summoning a deliberately salacious expression as he eyed the evening private-duty nurse that Georges had sent over from the agency. And then the older man appealed to Georges. "Get Vienna off my hands, will you, boy? If I give her half a chance, she will be cutting my food for me."

Georges laughed and slipped his arm around her waist, gently urging Vienna toward the door. He handed her the purse that was on the side table. "As long as she doesn't offer to chew it for you."

Amos made a face and shivered.

"We'll be back early," Vienna promised her grandfather just before crossing the threshold.

"Then I will be very disappointed in both of you," Amos declared with feeling. "Besides—" the old man raised and lowered his eyebrows comically "—if you come back too soon, you might be interrupting something."

Georges took that as an exit line and closed the door behind them. He led the way to the curb where he'd parked his newly detailed, gleaming red sports car.

Vienna's thoughts were still back in the living room. She frowned slightly. "I hope he's not too much of a handful for Silvia."

"Don't worry, she knows how to handle herself. She'll be fine." Lowering his mouth so that it was next to her ear, he assured her, "He'll be fine."

God, she hoped so. She looked at Georges, wanting desperately to have her mind set at ease. "Is that your professional opinion?"

"It is. Get it while it's hot." His smile widened as he opened the passenger-side door for her.

"Speaking of hot—" his eyes swept over her "—you look sensational in that dress."

Color rose to her cheeks. She got into the car. "Thank you."

She would look even more sensational without it, Georges caught himself thinking as he got behind the wheel. He glanced in her direction as he buckled his seat belt. Her belt was secured and her fingers were wrapped around her purse, allowing it to live up to the description: clutch purse. Her knuckles were all but white.

"He'll be all right," he repeated, turning on the ignition.

Vienna paused to blow out a breath before answering. "I'm not worried about that." It was a lie, but not a very big one. She knew she was being overly concerned about her grandfather and overly protective. But he *was* her only living relative and she did love the old man dearly. Independent though she was, she just couldn't picture life without him in it.

Georges wove his way out of her development. "Then what?"

There was no sense in lying about it. Even though she was looking forward to meeting the famous Lily Moreau, she couldn't help wondering what the woman would think of her. After all, she was sleeping with the woman's son—or, at least, had slept with him. Even though Lily didn't know that, it didn't change anything. She wanted the artist to like her.

But she couldn't say any of that to him. It would sound as if she were assuming too much. One step at a time.

"It's not every day I get to meet a living legend," she answered. Shifting in her seat to face him, she asked, "What's she like?"

"Mother?" Living legend. Funny, he had never thought of her in those terms. Even when he occasionally read stories about her, her shows, her three-day parties, he didn't really associate that person with the woman who, whenever she was in town, would tuck him into bed. "She's just Mother." Amused, Georges turned his head for a moment and smiled at her. "Don't worry, she doesn't eat people for dinner," he teased. "Only for breakfast."

"Very reassuring," she said wryly. And then her nervousness resurfaced. "No, really, tell me. What's she like?"

"A little larger than life, I guess. Enthusiastic. About everything," he added because it was true. He'd never known his mother to take things lightly or not jump into things with both feet. "You know that old classic line from that Bette Davis movie?" He fished for the title. "*All About somebody or other—*"

"Alice," Vienna supplied, then quickly amended, "No, I mean Eve. *All About Eve.*" She'd heard of it, but she'd never seen it. Was his mother shrewish and self-centered like the main character was supposed to be?

"Right," he said. "Anyway, in the movie Bette Davis says something like, 'Buckle up, it's going to be a bumpy night.'" He grinned. "I think Bette Davis knew my mother. With Mother you just never know what to expect."

"In other words, expect the unexpected."

"You've got it." As he got onto the freeway that eventually led to the gallery, Georges glanced at the woman in the passenger seat. She *did* look nervous, he thought. Maybe he shouldn't have invited her. Too late now. There was nothing left to do but try to reassure her. "Mother doesn't care for most women too much, but she'll love you."

"Why?"

He laughed then and the rich, mellow sound warmed her. "How could she not?"

Her breath stopped traveling again. It seemed to be a regular occurrence every time she was around him. Or thought about him. Vienna looked at his profile to see if he was joking, or just turning on the charm that came to him as easily as breathing did for some.

They came to a red light and he pressed down on the brake. As if sensing that she was studying him, Georges spared her a long glance.

He seemed serious, she realized. Was he? Or was

that just his way of putting her at her ease? In either case, she was appreciative. But she needed more.

"You won't leave my side?" she asked.

"Stick to it like glue," he vowed. "Unless, of course, you want to use the ladies' room. If I go in with you, there might be a problem." He grinned again, and her stomach flipped.

The light changed and he moved his foot back on the accelerator.

Just the sound of his voice was reassuring, she thought. "What if I go into the ladies' room and your mother walks in after me?"

He never hesitated. "Run."

And then he laughed, making her feel infinitely better. As if she could do anything, face anything. As long as he was there with her. How had he become so important to her so quickly? A few weeks ago, she hadn't even known he existed. Moreover, she'd been firm in her resolve to leave things like love hidden away on some back shelf, completely out of sight.

And now…

And now there it was, she realized, front and center. Love.

Oh my God—she loved him?

The realization—the very thought—had nerves jumping through her again. It took a great deal of effort on her part to bank them all down before they finally reached the gallery.

* * *

The Sunrise Gallery was one very large room that faced the street. It had cathedral ceilings and stark white walls that were repainted on a regular basis. The snow-white walls acted as a dramatic backdrop for the paintings that continually found their way through the front door.

Right now, the gallery was crammed with patrons, would-be patrons and Lily's well-wishers. It was a gathering of the famous, the not-so-famous and the wealthy unknowns. Smoking had long since been banned from the city's buildings but the air was thick with voices.

When Georges opened the front door for her, the wall of sound hit Vienna hard. She was tempted to hang back. "I didn't realize that there'd be so many people," she confessed.

Georges took her hand and crossed the threshold. The door closed behind them, sealing them in. "Neither did I. Looks like Mother went all out spreading the word."

Slipping his hand around her waist reassuringly, Georges guided her away from the entrance and toward the displays.

Vienna looked at him curiously. "Can't imagine why she'd have to. The very mention of her paintings would bring people in."

"Oh, this isn't a showing of her paintings."

Vienna didn't understand. She looked at the small grouping of abstract paintings closest to her. "Then whose—"

"Her...friend's." Stuck for the right term, he pulled the all-purpose label into service. "Kyle Winterset or Summerfield or some such name involving one of the seasons."

"Autumn," Alain said, coming up behind them. He clamped down one hand on his brother's shoulder. The other held a glass of champagne. A half-empty glass of champagne. His eyes shifted to the woman beside his brother. The interest was impossible to miss. "His name is Kyle Autumn."

Georges didn't remember hearing that last name. Had to be a last-minute decision of his mother's. "You're kidding."

Wearing a tuxedo like his brother, Alain lifted his broad shoulders in a careless shrug. "That's what Mother says." He gestured toward a far wall with his glass. "Some of his efforts aren't half-bad." Taking a sip of champagne, he smiled into his glass. "Of course, his efforts with Mother are spectacular." Lowering the glass again, he looked at Vienna. "Hello. My uncouth brother seems to have completely forgotten his manners and lost the ability to speak, so while he's just standing there, posing for the park's next statue, let me do the honors and introduce myself. I'm Alain Dulac, Georges' younger brother." Lifting her hand, he brought it to his lips in the courtly fashion of an era long gone. And then he raised his eyes to hers. "And you are…?"

"Not impressed," Georges informed him before Vienna could reply. Taking possession of his younger brother's arm, he drew Alain away from Vienna.

"Territorial," Alain commented, nodding with approval as he looked from his brother to the woman in shimmering blue. "Sounds promising." Moving closer to her, Alain said in a stage whisper, "He's never brought any of his ladies to one of Mother's shows."

Georges took matters into his own hands. If he didn't, he had a feeling that Alain would feel tempted to monopolize Vienna all night. Not that he could blame him.

"Go fill up your glass, Alain," Georges urged. Turning his brother away from Vienna, he placed both hands on Alain's shoulders and propelled him toward a waiter. The latter was moving through the crowd, offering glasses of champagne to those without liquid libation. "Alone" again, he focused on Vienna. "Don't mind Alain," he told her. "He likes to run off at the mouth. He's a lawyer, so it's pretty much an occupational hazard."

She'd liked Alain, she thought. And the two got on like typical brothers. An only child, she envied Georges a little. "He seems nice."

Georges made a sound that was swallowed up by the crowd's noise. "Operative word here being *seems*."

Well, one hurdle passed without incident. But Alain wasn't the main attraction. Vienna drew in a breath. "When do I get to meet your mother?"

"Now." He barely had time to utter the single word—or was it more of a warning?—before Lily swooped down on them.

Vienna swung around in time to see a diminutive, shapely woman with raven-black hair and eyes the color of violets in the spring materialize behind her. Her nails and lips were scarlet. The rest of her was all in black.

On her, black seemed like a lively color.

"Welcome, welcome," Lily declared with the dramatic intonation she was famous for. Not standing on ceremony, she enveloped Vienna in an embrace, pressing her against an ample chest that would have been more in keeping with a far larger woman. "I'm Lily and you must be…?" She looked from Vienna to her son, waiting for a name. Wanting to have been filled in yesterday.

"Vienna Hollenbeck," Georges said, which was good because she seemed to have temporarily lost her voice.

"Vienna," Lily echoed. And then she nodded her approval. "What a charming name." Releasing her, Lily took half a step back and extended her hand to her. "Well, I'm Lily Moreau," she said needlessly, as if she could be anyone else. "Georges' mother."

Not foremost, Georges thought. Lily had never been just a mother to any of them. It had always seemed more like a footnote, an afterthought, even though she'd always been careful to see that they were well cared for. But he was beginning to think that maybe Philippe was right. Lily seemed to be trying to make up for a huge amount of lost time.

Well, if anyone could do it, Lily could.

Turning away from them for a moment, Lily extended her hand to someone just behind her, beckoning to him with her fingertips. Scarlet spiders moving through the air.

When he joined her, she slipped both her arms through his and smiled. Damn, but she seemed content, Georges thought. When had she last looked like that?

"And this is Kyle Autumn," she was saying to Vienna. "My protégé."

So that was what they were calling it these days, Georges thought. Kyle was tall and thin, with jet-black hair. He wore a black turtleneck sweater and black slacks, looking for all the world like a throwback to the beat era of the fifties. But his mother had a penchant for black and he had a feeling that Kyle did everything in his power to please her and remain on Lily's good side.

He refused to think about how far Kyle's efforts extended.

Kyle towered over the famed artist. "And she is my muse, my angel," Kyle told them. The statement was punctuated by a light kiss pressed against the top of Lily's head.

Georges experienced a sudden desire to punch that very good-looking jaw, but refrained.

Oblivious to her son's thoughts, Lily seemed appropriately pleased by Kyle's words. "Kyle, you know my son, Georges. This—" scarlet fingertips gestured toward Vienna "—is Vienna Hollenbeck, his…"

Lily let her voice trail off, waiting for one of them to fill in the glaring blank she'd left open.

Instinctively, she knew that Georges would want to avoid any labels being thrown at whatever it was they had between them. So Vienna took the conversation in a different direction. "Dr. Armand is my grandfather's doctor. He saved his life," she told Lily, then added, "And mine."

Very carefully sculpted eyebrows narrowed over dramatic eyes. Lily seemed to be looking right into her. "Is that figuratively, or literally?"

Both, Vienna thought. But out loud, she replied, "Literally."

The answer seemed to please the mother in Lily.

"I need to hear all about it," Lily declared, slipping her arm through Vienna's.

Georges almost laughed. For a fleeting moment, the expression on Vienna's face looked as if she were being kidnapped by a hoard of Vikings and whisked off to the deck of their ship as their booty.

"Shouldn't you be mingling with your other guests?" Georges suggested tactfully. He glanced at the so-called guest of honor. "Introducing them to Kyle's work?"

To his surprise, when his mother glanced at him, there was gratitude in her smile.

She thinks I've accepted him, Georges realized. When had his opinion, or the opinion of his brothers, mattered to her? He loved his mother and he was certain, in her own fashion, she loved all of them, but he had never thought of her as the garden variety mother who wanted to matter to her children or who sought their approval, however covertly. This was something new.

Lily clapped her hands together, suddenly struck by a thought, her subtle interrogation of Vienna, for the moment, placed on hold. "I almost forgot, Georges. I have a gift for you."

He looked at her, a little stunned. "A gift? Why? What's the occasion?" Gifts came on birthdays and Christmas. Tons of them. Sometimes even in the right size. Lily was generous and lavish, though thoughtful rarely ever entered into it.

"Your graduation from the residency program," she declared, her expression asking how he could have possibly forgotten that.

"That's not for another few months, Mother," he tactfully reminded her.

Undaunted, she waved her hand at the reminder. "So, I'm a little early. Why wait until the last minute?" She turned toward the tall, handsome man beside her. "Kyle, be a darling and bring me the box from the back room."

Georges knew for a fact that the "back room" was actually the office where the owner of the gallery conducted his day-to-day business. But, as they all knew, when his mother moved in, she commandeered everything in her path and it all became hers.

He watched as his mother looked after Kyle as he disappeared from view. Like a schoolgirl watching her first crush, he thought. He wondered how concerned he and his brothers should be.

Kyle returned quickly, carrying a large rectangular box before him. When he brought it to her, Lily shook her head.

"Not to me, to him." She pointed at her son. Shifting, Kyle presented the large box to Georges. "Open it," Lily coaxed, sounding very much like an eager child on Christmas morning. "Open it."

Curious now himself, Georges did as she requested. Silver wrapping rained down to his feet as he tore it away. Vienna held the bottom of the box for him as he lifted the lid and found himself looking down at—

"A defibrillator?" he asked, looking up at Lily quizzically.

His mother nodded. "You want to be a heart surgeon, don't you?" she asked, obviously proud that she remembered. And then uncertainty entered her eyes. "Or have you changed your mind?"

"No, I haven't changed my mind," he assured her, looking back down at the box and its contents again. Heart surgery was his eventual goal, but that was going to require two more years of residency, hopefully again at Blair.

"Then this is perfect for you," she declared, then flashed a pleased smile.

They had the same smile, Vienna thought.

"This way," Lily was saying to him, "if my heart stops beating, you can zap me back to the land of the living without my having to go to that wretched hospital." To Lily, all hospitals were wretched and meant to be avoided at all costs. She beamed at him. It was the most expensive one she could find. "Do you like it?" she wanted to know. "Tell me you like it. If you don't, I can always exchange it for—"

He didn't even want to imagine what was running through her head. "I like it, Mother, I like it," he told her with the feeling he knew she required. Holding on to his gift, he stooped to kiss her cheek. "You're one of a kind."

"Yes, I know," she replied, looking pleased with herself. Forgetting about the inquest she'd wanted to conduct, Lily turned to Kyle. "Now we can go and mingle, my love."

Still holding the box with the defibrillator in it, Georges eyed Vienna to see how she'd weathered her first encounter with his mother.

"She's a little like a hurricane," he repeated his earlier description. "If you're left standing in her wake, you're doing well."

That, Vienna thought, was a gross understatement.

Chapter Thirteen

Once she realized that there was nothing to be nervous about, Vienna had a wonderful time at the gallery.

She had an even better time afterward.

Given Georges' careless-charmer reputation and the intimate level of their present relationship, it surprised Vienna that he took nothing for granted when it came to her feelings. After spending a good twenty minutes saying goodbye to his mother and her protégé, his brother Alain and the man's date, and his brother Philippe, who was there with his fiancée, Janice, as well as Janice's sparkling jewel of a daughter, Kelli, Georges escorted her out of the gallery. Taking her arm, he hustled her across the parking lot and to his sports car.

Just as he unlocked and opened the passenger-side door for her, he surprised her by whispering against her hair, "I know you want to get back to your grandfather, but why don't you make a call to Silvia and see how he's doing?"

"Why?"

She searched his face, wondering if he knew something she didn't. Had Georges gotten a call from the nurse while she was talking to Janice or one of the other patrons at the gallery? Had he kept it to himself, not wanting to spoil her time? The nerves she'd successfully eradicated earlier came rushing back.

But Georges seemed untroubled. "Because I thought if he was doing well, maybe we wouldn't have to call an end to the evening so soon."

Relieved, she glanced at her watch. "It's not evening anymore. It's very early morning."

"Semantics," he responded, amused. Once inside the vehicle, he looked at her to gauge her feelings. "Does that mean you don't want to stop at my place for a nightcap?"

She wasn't interested in a nightcap, but she was interested in his place. She'd never seen where he lived before. The fact that he wanted to bring her there was a large step forward.

"Maybe just for a few minutes," Vienna allowed, doing her best not to sound as excited as she felt. As she took out her cell phone, she saw that he was grinning. "What?"

"What I have in mind might take a little longer than just a few minutes." His eyes were teasing her as he buckled up. "Unless we *really* hurry."

She couldn't have restrained the smile that rose to her lips even if she'd been sucking on a lemon. "Maybe for more than a few minutes," she amended.

He put the car in gear. "Sounds good to me."

And it was good. Oh, so good. For both of them.

So good, she thought later, that the very word needed a new meaning, one that took in the presence of flashing lights, electrical currents flowing through limbs and a complete spectrum of adjectives that bowed before the altar of ecstasy.

They'd made love now more than a few times, and each time was better than the last. Almost different from the last. It still surprised her that she could experience this heightened state of pleasure. Lovemaking with Edward had been nice. Satisfying most of the time, but after the first time, it had become almost routine to the point that she worried about her own response. She knew what to expect. Edward made love by the numbers.

If Edward played the kazoo, Georges was the

whole damn orchestra, she thought. She'd quickly discovered that she never knew *what* to expect. There was always the promise of something new, something wondrous each and every time they made love together.

He taught her that she could climax in a myriad of ways, enjoy a myriad of sensations, all slightly different from one another. And she never, *ever* knew which she would experience.

Or for how long. Some climaxes tiptoed in before pouncing, others exploded with a teeth-jarring crescendo and then softly slipped away. Still others seemed to go on and on for so long, she thought she was going to expire from sheer sweet agony.

But covertly woven through the pleasure was the dreaded realization that a man like this was not going to stay. A man like this would, sooner or later, find himself straying to new ground, in search of new conquests.

Vienna was on borrowed time, and she knew it.

The knowledge made her try to savor everything as much as she could, to make love with him in the fullest sense of the word. It helped her not to think about the future.

She couldn't help but think of the future.

Turning toward her on his bed as the euphoria of their last joining began to fade away, Georges saw the sadness in her eyes before she had a chance to bank it down. "What's the matter?"

Vienna forced a smile to her lips, but it was just that. Forced. "Nothing."

He traced the outline of her lips with his fingertip. "Nothing was making you frown, hence it has to be something."

When she said nothing in response, Georges pressed his lips to her bare shoulder. She had to struggle not to shiver, not to turn into him and just cling. The last thing a man such as Georges wanted was someone clinging to him like some hapless damsel in distress. Besides, that wasn't her, she silently insisted. What was going on? She was more independent than that.

Wasn't she?

Because he was still waiting for an answer, she gave him a half truth. "You know when you're very, very happy and you feel it just can't last? That something is going to happen to take that happiness away from you?"

She was thinking of her grandfather, Georges thought. Afraid that the yin and yang of life would take the man from her because she was enjoying herself too much. It wasn't a philosophy he ascribed to.

"It doesn't always have to be that way," he told her, slipping his arms around her waist and pulling her body into his. He did his best to look serious.

"There are documented cases of some people experiencing happiness for decades."

"You're making that up." And she loved him for it, she thought. Loved him for trying to joke her out of it, for trying to make her feel better instead of annoyed that she was marring his own enjoyment.

"You'll have to torture me to get me to admit that," he told her.

"All right," she agreed. "How shall I start?"

Vienna got no further in her teasing. He'd framed her face with his hands and brought her mouth down to his, stealing her breath—and her heart—away again.

Maybe he was right, Vienna thought two weeks later as she glanced over her shoulder toward the dining room. Maybe Georges had actually been right, even though he'd been teasing, and there were cases of happiness that had lasted for decades. Because God knew, she was close to deliriously happy and fervently praying that she would remain that way.

Moving about the kitchen quickly, Vienna deposited the empty beer bottles into the recycling bag and gathered together another eight bottles from the refrigerator. She placed them on the tray.

Voices crisscrossed over one another from the other room, warming her.

Holding her breath, she picked up the tray and walked slowly into the dining room, which had been commandeered tonight by Philippe, Georges, Alain, Gordon and three of their cousins whom she'd met at the gallery show last week: Vinnie, Remy and Beau. Seemingly out of the blue, Georges had suggested to her that he and the others bring their weekly poker game over here. Specifically to her grandfather. He'd broached the idea within Amos's hearing range. The old man had perked up considerably and was overjoyed at the prospect of having so much testosterone gathered together under his roof.

She, on the other hand, although thrilled by the thought of her grandfather having company, hadn't exactly been keen on the idea of having him gamble. He wasn't really all that good. But then Georges had explained that they bet with toothpicks, not money, and that the big winner collected a prize, a chore of his choosing performed by the big loser of the evening.

That was right up her grandfather's alley.

Miraculously enough, Vienna noted as she set down the tray on the side table, her grandfather seemed to be winning. She began to distribute the bottles, wondering if her grandfather's winning streak was due to luck or design.

"How's it going?" she asked cheerfully, placing

an opened bottle before Philippe and then another before Alain.

Georges frowned as he made a show of studying his hand. "You didn't tell me that in another life, your grandfather was a riverboat gambler."

"Just lucky." Amos chuckled. He looked as pleased as a child at Christmas who'd discovered Santa Claus's bag of toys.

She paused in her bottle distribution to plant a kiss on the crown of his snow-white head. "You always were that," she agreed affectionately.

Looking back at the table, he patted the hand that had dropped to his shoulder. "I was to have gotten you as my granddaughter."

Taking a last long look at his hand as Amos placed another bet, Alain blew out a breath and folded his cards. "Well, I'm out."

Vinnie followed suit, tossing down his hand. "Me, too."

"Call," Philippe said, tossing in the same number of toothpicks that Amos had used to raise the stacks.

A show of the remaining cards around the table had Amos being the big winner again. The old man beamed as he drew the colorful assortment to tooth-picks to himself, adding to his pile.

Smiling to herself, Vienna took her empty tray and retreated to the kitchen.

"I'm going to sit the next hand out," Georges announced, rising.

Walking into the kitchen, he found Vienna working at the counter, making another batch of sandwiches. She'd been feeding them all night. He'd already told her that she didn't have to do that, but he couldn't seem to get her to pay attention. The lady had a mind of her own, he thought fondly.

"Need any help?" he asked.

Taking a long serrated bread knife, she cut the sandwich she'd just completed in half. She noted Gordon had been wolfing them down as if he hadn't eaten in days. Losing made him hungry, she thought.

Placing the sandwich on a plate, she turned from the counter and reached for a towel to wipe her fingers. "You've already done plenty," she told him.

"All I did was lose a bunch of blue and green toothpicks. And a couple of gold ones," he recalled. Coming up behind her, he slipped his arms around her waist, enjoying the way they seemed to fit together no matter what the angle. Resting his cheek against the top of her head, he paused to inhale the fragrance of her shampoo. It made him think of wildflowers. "Your grandfather's one sharp player."

Vienna laughed shortly. "And you, sir, are one really poor liar." Discarding the towel, she turned around to face him, her body brushing against his, sending electrical pulses through them both. "I would have thought that a man with a harem of women in his past history would be a better liar than that."

"Whoa, what harem?" he asked, looking properly indignant. "No harem, Vienna. I'm as innocent as a lamb." Georges did his best to look simple and unworldly.

She only laughed. The man had probably ceased being innocent the second he'd hit puberty. Rather than strands of jealousy, she felt only affection.

"The hell you are." She threaded her arms around his neck. Ever so subtly, her body leaned into his. "You've made him very happy, Georges. I can't tell you what that means to me."

He nodded solemnly. "There are times when words fail." And then, unable to keep a straight face any longer, he laughed as his eyes shone. "Maybe you can show me later instead."

"I'd be happy to."

The counter at her back, Vienna rose up on her toes, her eyes never leaving his. She kissed him then, long and hard and with an endless gratitude that seemed to spill out and go on spilling. When they drew apart for a breath, she could still feel her heart swelling with the affection she felt.

"I love you." The next moment, to her horror, her

words came echoing back to her. Her eyes widened in shock as she looked up at him, trying to read his reaction. God, but she hadn't meant to say that. Nothing drove a man away faster than hearing those words prematurely. "Sorry," she apologized quickly. Vienna could feel her throat tightening up as a panic threatened to set in. "That just slipped out. I tend to say 'I love you' when I'm very happy. It doesn't mean anything, really," she assured him with a wee bit too much feeling.

Didn't it? he wondered. Looking into her eyes, he found he couldn't tell. She'd suddenly masked her feelings from him.

"That's a shame," he told her. "Because it sounded nice."

He'd never had a woman tell him that before. That she loved him. Partly because, he surmised, he had never stayed around long enough for a woman to feel the kind of emotions that would prompt her to say that. Until this very moment, he'd always thought himself lucky not to be entangled in that sort of web, where basic feelings came out to play and wound up complicating everything they came in contact with.

Maybe he was wrong, Georges thought now as he looked down into her face.

Maybe he hadn't been lucky not to hear it. Because hearing her say she loved him had stirred something inside him, something that had been dormant—possibly forever.

He wasn't really sure what to do with this new feeling, but he knew it bore closer scrutiny.

Had she upset him? Was he serious? She hadn't a clue. Her best bet, she decided, was to be philosophical, because she had absolutely no idea what kind of ground she was standing on, whether it was rock solid or oatmeal soft.

"Well, it certainly does sound nicer than hearing someone shout, 'I hate you,'" she agreed. The tips of her fingers grew damp. Time to change the subject quick, she thought, before there turned out to be no way out.

She cleared her throat and nodded toward the large rectangular box she had on the far end of the counter. She'd brought it home with her from the bakery. Very carefully, she removed her arms from around his neck and took a step away. She picked up the sandwich she'd just made for Gordon. "Since you want to help, why don't you carry that box in for me?"

He went to do as she asked. The box was huge. Georges glanced at her over his shoulder. "Another defibrillator?" he teased. "I've still got the one my mother gave me in the trunk of my car."

He'd been meaning to put it away since the night at the gallery, but somehow, he never thought of it until well after he was already home and in bed, usually exhausted beyond words after putting in double shifts at the hospital.

"No, something some people might say necessitates having a defibrillator in the trunk of your car." She paused to point at the logo on the side of the box. It was a drawing of a girl munching a jelly donut. Her grandfather had once told her he'd given a photo of her at age four to an artist and this was what he had designed. "Pastries," she told him.

He picked up the box, ready to follow her out. "I knew that."

Coming back into the dining room again, Vienna was greeted by the sound of her grandfather's laughter as the man responded to something Philippe said to him. It warmed her heart.

"Thanks," Gordon said heartily as she placed a roast beef sandwich before him.

She smiled her response, then looked at the other faces around the oval table. "All right, gentlemen," she announced, "whenever you're ready, there are pastries from my grandfather's bakery awaiting your pleasure." Once Georges placed the box on the side table, she removed the lid to expose more than twenty different kinds of confection.

She could almost hear everyone's mouth watering.

"*Our* bakery," Amos corrected, raising his voice as he looked at her pointedly. "Everything that's mine is yours, Vienna, you know that."

She pretended to eye the colorful mass of tooth-picks gathered on the table before him. "Including your toothpicks?" she teased.

Without realizing it, she slanted a look toward Georges. If she were the evening's big winner and he the loser, she knew exactly what she'd ask for as her prize.

A huge, pleased grin slipped over her grand-father's face. His color had completely returned and he looked exactly the way she always thought of him, exactly the way he had looked when he had first come into her life to take care of her.

"*Almost* everything," Amos amended. And then he took on his rightful role as host, gesturing toward the box of pastries. "Please," he urged his guests, "eat up and then we will continue play-ing." His expression was positively mischievous as he added, "I have leaves in my gutters that need removing."

His mouth full of a cruller, Vinnie glanced at Vienna. "Is that some kind of Austrian idiom?"

"Only for those Austrians with rain gutters," she deadpanned.

And then she laughed as Georges came up behind her and wrapped his arms around her in a bear hug. Out of the corner of her eye, she saw the contented look on her grandfather's face as he sat back in his chair, observing them.

He looked happy, she thought. Maybe happiness *could* go on indefinitely.

At least she could hope.

Chapter Fourteen

"He's in his element, and he's happy."

Abruptly breaking the silence and the rhythm of slow, easy breathing that came after lovemaking, Vienna began talking to Georges about her grandfather.

Though he'd asked after the man's health, Georges hardly heard her. His own thoughts were filling up the spaces in his head.

They were lying on his bed. An initial outing that had the preview of a new, Broadway-bound play at its core had somehow morphed into this, another wild, tempestuous meeting of the body and the soul.

It was not the first time they'd gotten sidetracked like this. The exceedingly enjoyable interlude just further fueled the realization that, after six weeks together—hardly a lifetime—Vienna Hollenbeck was swiftly becoming the center of his universe, something that had never happened to him before, and certainly not to this degree.

It also brought home the fact that he needed to get out—now—before there was no turning back. Before he stood there naked in the town square, waiting to be incinerated. Because he knew, by example, that it could happen.

"But I can't help feeling that he's doing too much," Vienna was saying. "He refuses to take things slow, no matter what I say. He went back full-time last week, working hours like he used to. All his customers were thrilled to see him, and he looked like a kid at Christmas." She caught her lower lip between her teeth, still staring up at the ceiling, trying to find a way to bank down her fears. About everything. "Ordinarily, I'd say that was the best medicine in the world for him, but—"

It took a beat for him to realize that she'd stopped talking. That, her voice trailing off, she'd turned to look at him.

She was waiting for him to say something. He replayed her words in his head as best he could. There were gaps. "You're worried about him."

"That's what I've been saying."

Georges' response bothered her. He wasn't here tonight, she thought. Even at the height of their lovemaking, when she felt as if the very walls were catching fire, she'd had this distant, uneasy sense that part of him wasn't there with her. That hadn't happened before.

The beginning of the end? Vienna wondered.

All along, amid her happiness, she'd been dreading this. Anticipating this. Pretending it wasn't going to come, knowing that it would because he was who he was. She was a nester and he was a man who moved from hotel to hotel. In her heart, she'd always known that she was just a stop along his route.

When in doubt, make doctor noises, Georges thought. Besides, though the last exam had been excellent, Vienna might have a point. Her grandfather might be having some kind of relapse. No sense in taking a chance.

"Bring him by the hospital tomorrow," he said. "I can have a few tests done." He smiled at her. "Put your fears to rest."

Not that easy, she said silently. In either case. But out loud, she only focused on one concern. "He'll say he's too busy."

Georges smiled. "If anyone can make him, you can. Besides, I'm his doctor. And he likes me."

She did her best not to let him sense the tension that all but snapped through her veins. "Yes, he does."

And so do I, God help me. So much that I can hardly breathe. How am I going to stand it when you go?

Georges took in a long breath and glanced at his watch. "Well, our little detour cost us the play. Sorry about that," he apologized. "No sense in walking in on the last third—unless you want to," he tagged on, giving her the option.

But she shook her head. "No, that's all right," Vienna murmured.

"We still have late reservations at the restaurant," he remembered. "We could easily make that."

Whatever appetite she'd had had fled in the wake of this uneasiness. "No, I'm not really hungry. Maybe we should just call it a night."

If he'd had his head caught in a cement mixer, he would have still picked up on the desolation in her voice. Georges sat up. "Something wrong?"

Now there's an understatement. The smile that curved her mouth was the epitome of sadness even though she tried hard to lock her feelings away. "Depends if you're you or me."

Something was very wrong here, Georges thought. Was she clairvoyant despite her protests? Had she picked up on something, on the thoughts shuffling through his head? He didn't want to hurt her for the world. He just didn't want to hurt himself, either. "I'm not sure I follow."

"Because you don't follow, you lead." Vienna sat up, too, and as she did, she reached for the clothes that had been haphazardly tossed aside in the frantic quest for fulfillment and fleeting ecstasy. "Look, we both know that this is just an interlude." She got out of bed. "A wonderful, wonderful interlude, at least for me, but it's not the beginning of something." Vienna turned to face him, regal in her stance despite the fact that the only clothing she had on was what she was holding against her. Her eyes held his for a moment. "When this is over—" she couldn't bring herself to pronounce its demise just yet "—I want you to tell me. I don't want you here a moment longer than you want to be."

He wished he could somehow reassure her even as he wanted to back away. "What brought this on?"

"You." Vienna held her clothes tighter, as if that could somehow keep her from crying. "I can feel you withdrawing."

God, she knew him better than he knew himself, he thought.

Very softly, she told him, "I just want you to know I understand." Vienna looked away, afraid that she was going to break down. There was an emptiness hovering on the edges of her being, threatening to leap forward and swallow her up if she didn't keep moving, didn't keep sidestepping it somehow. "I'd like to go home now, if you don't mind."

Vienna didn't wait for his answer. Instead, she went into his bathroom and shut the door. When she came out five minutes later, he was already dressed. He wasn't trying to talk her out of it. Wasn't even trying to deny what she'd guessed. Which meant that she was right.

It was over.

She was making it easy for him. She knew that. But then, she didn't want to cling to him. It wouldn't mean anything that way. The only way she wanted him in her life was if he truly wanted to be there. And it was obvious that he didn't.

The ride home was filled with music from the radio, but it didn't block out the silence within the car. The silence encroaching like a malevolent force, feeding on itself.

Vienna was painfully aware of it. Painfully aware that for the first time since she'd met him, Georges wasn't talking to her, wasn't making her laugh or feel better about a given situation. His silence was agreement. She'd never hated being right so much in her life.

The ache inside her grew with every passing moment, every passing mile. And then they were at her door. He pulled the car up at the curb in front of her mailbox.

She had her hand on the door handle, ready to leap from the car. "You don't have to come out," she protested, but he did anyway.

He still wasn't sure what had happened, how this had evolved out of some of the most satisfying love-making he'd ever experienced. Either he was transparent to her, he decided, or she really was clairvoyant.

In either case, he wasn't just going to eject her out of the vehicle and take off. "I'm walking you to your door," he told her firmly.

Maybe this was a mistake. Even though part of him was grateful to her for making it so easy for him, for giving him an escape hatch, part of him felt an incredible, overwhelming sadness descend over him, the magnitude of which he'd never dealt with before. The sadness told him that maybe it already was too late. Maybe this one had come to mean more to him than anyone before her and that he'd be a fool to leave her.

Damn, up was down and down was up, and he'd lost his compass.

His course of action with women had always been so clear-cut, so natural for him before now. He'd never been confused before, never had his emotions tied up in knots before. Because no one had ever meant more than just having a good time and living in the moment.

He wanted more. He wanted lots of moments.

Damn it, go! Go before you make the biggest mistake of your life, a voice in his head ordered urgently, even as he walked her to the door.

"I was serious about you bringing him in tomorrow," he told her.

Vienna nodded, valiantly trying to concentrate on her grandfather and his health, and nothing more. Amos Schwarzwalden deserved nothing less from her and she was going to wrap herself up in her responsibilities and duties, using them to help her get over this.

She tried her best not to allow her voice to sound shaky. "I'll get in touch with you after I have a chance to talk to my grandfather."

Georges nodded. Guilt, indecision and sorrow dueled madly within him, gluing him in place.

"Vienna—" he began, not knowing what he was going to say after that.

There was no need to worry. She was already turning away. A second later, she'd let herself into the house, closing the door behind her.

Georges stood for a moment, staring at the door, wondering if he should make an excuse to knock and ask her to let him come in. But then he took a breath and turned away. He began to walk to his car.

It was better this way. Better for him, for her.

Better that he should—

He heard the door swing open and then bang on the opposite wall as Vienna screamed out his name. His heart froze.

Instantly, he came running back to her. He knew without being told that the look on her face had nothing to do with what had just happened between them.

"It's my grandfather." Her throat was so tight with fear, she could hardly get the words out, hardly get any air in. "This way—"

Clamping on to his hand, she ran back so fast, she was all but dragging him in her wake.

Amos was in the kitchen, lying facedown and unconscious on the floor.

"He's not breathing," she sobbed. "I tried to make him breathe, but I can't."

Dropping to his knees, Georges dug into his pocket. He threw her his car keys. "I've still got that defibrillator in the trunk of my car." Silently he blessed his mother. "Get it," he ordered as he began manual CPR.

Trembling, Vienna missed the keys when he threw them. Picking them up, she dashed outside. She was back almost before she left.

"Here," she cried, dropping to her knees beside him with the defibrillator in her arms. "Do something," she begged. "Bring him back." She knew how unreasonable that sounded, but she didn't want to be reasonable; she wanted to be a granddaughter. Amos's granddaughter.

"I'm trying, Vienna, I'm trying. Plug it in," he told her.

Once the defibrillator was sufficiently charged and up and running, Georges picked up the paddles.

"Call 911," he told her. "He's going to have to go back to the hospital."

For a split second, she felt paralyzed. She could only stare at what Georges was doing. "But he's going to be all right, isn't he? Isn't he?" she demanded.

"I'm doing my best," he shouted. "Now make the damn call!"

By the time she'd gotten the dispatch's promise to send an ambulance right away, Georges had gotten her grandfather's heartbeat back.

Rocking back on his heels, feeling more drained than the man lying before him, Georges told her, "It's beating again."

She didn't realize she was crying until then. Her cheeks were wet and a teardrop fell on her collarbone. She wanted to throw herself over her grandfather, to hold him close to her and will her life force into his. But she was afraid if she did, the jarring motion might do something to change the status quo.

She was afraid to even breathe.

Moving forward, she took the old man's hand in hers. "You live, you hear me, old man?" she instructed through gritted teeth. She had to blink twice in order to see him. Her eyes were filling up with tears. "You can't leave me to handle everything, Grandpa. It's not fair. I need you. You have to live. I need you," she repeated, her voice breaking.

She could have sworn she saw the tiniest of smiles curve the old man's lips just then.

He'd heard her, she thought, clinging to that thought as if it were a life preserver in a choppy, erratic ocean. He'd heard her. He was going to live. Never once had her grandfather denied her anything she'd asked for.

Her grandfather was going to be all right. She wouldn't let him not be.

The diagnosis came as no surprise. Amos had had a massive heart attack. Although they'd gotten his heart to begin beating on its own again, the coma he'd slipped into continued, mocking every effort Georges attempted to bring him around.

One day came and went, bringing another in its wake. There was no change in Amos's condition. Vienna sat by his side, keeping vigil. Other people came to the hospital to visit him, a great many people. Raul had put out the word that the friendly

Austrian baker had taken a turn for the worse after seemingly being on the mend.

Because Amos had been placed in the coronary care unit for proper monitoring, visitors were supposedly restricted to two per hour for a total of five minutes each. No one paid attention to the rules. The nurses complained to them, to Vienna and to the doctor, all to no avail. Eventually, since the visitors were quiet and respectful, if persistent, the nurses surrendered.

And through it all, there was a growing concern not only for the comatose patient, but for the young woman who sat, waiflike, holding his hand, talking to him and praying.

Unable to cast a blind eye to what was happening before her any longer, the head day nurse, Chantal Reese, a twenty-six-year hospital veteran, not to mention the grandmother of five, decided to voice her opinion. Placing her ample figure in his path before Georges could walk down the corridor to Amos' sroom, she completely stopped him in his tracks.

He looked at her quizzically. "Something wrong, Chantal?"

"Yes, something's wrong. It's that girl."

"Girl?" he repeated.

"The old man's granddaughter." Before he could ask what she was talking about, she told him. "Dr. Armand, in the last three days, she's hardly moved out of that chair. Lord knows I haven't seen her eat anything, just drink a little water now and again. She's going to need one of our beds herself soon if she keeps this up." Though the other nurses swore the woman ate new hires for lunch on a regular basis, there was nothing but compassion in Chantal's wide, dark face. "Can't you talk any sense into her?"

He'd been concerned about Vienna himself. But every time he thought of telling her to go home, something in her eyes forbade him from making the suggestion. Over the last three days, she had been getting progressively more fragile.

"I can try," he told the nurse. "But she's a very stubborn young woman."

Chantal snorted, waving a dismissive hand at his protest. "Never known any woman who wouldn't listen to you once you got that sweet tongue of yours in gear, Dr. A." She gave him a knowing look.

"You give me way too much credit," he told her as he began to walk away.

"Not from what I hear." Her words followed him down the corridor.

That, he thought, was all behind him. Though he hadn't had much interaction with Vienna these last three days, except at her grandfather's bedside, he found himself in a kind of limbo. Free to resume the life he'd once led but with absolutely no inclination to do so.

Georges walked into the small cubicle allotted each patient within CCU. There was hardly enough room for proper maneuvering. At the moment, space was being taken up by a myriad of machines that kept tabs on every vital function the human body offered up for viewing.

Vienna was in a chair beside her grandfather's bed, holding his hand just the way she had been every other time he'd walked in. For a moment, she seemed oblivious to him. She was talking to Amos as if he was just asleep rather than comatose.

Chantal was right, he thought. Vienna's face appeared to be getting gaunt.

Just as he was about to say something to her, Vienna raised her eyes to his. "He won't wake up," she told him. Her voice was so incredibly sad that it threatened to break his heart. Letting out a ragged breath, she gazed back to the old man in the bed. "I shouldn't have left him." Each syllable was so pregnant with guilt.

"When?" According to Chantal and the other nurses on duty, Vienna hadn't left the old man's side for more than a few minutes in three days.

She pressed her lips together, trying to gain control over herself, over her voice. "The night we were supposed to see the play. I shouldn't have left him," she repeated. Despite her best efforts, a tear slipped down her cheek. She wiped it away with the back of her hand. "If I'd been there—"

"He would have still had his heart attack," Georges told her firmly.

He refrained from putting his arms around her, although the urge was strong. Ever since her grandfather had been brought there, it was as if she was steeling herself against any human contact. All her energy seemed to be focused on being with her grandfather. On willing him to health.

"But I could have gotten help for him faster. Who knows how long he was on the floor like that before I found him?" she sobbed.

Precious minutes could make the difference between life and death. She'd heard that over and over again. She'd been berating herself these last three days, wondering when her grandfather'd had his attack. Was it when she was making love with Georges? When he was undressing her? When they lay there in each other's arms?

If he died, she was never going to forgive herself for failing him. For putting her pleasure above his health. She'd known he wasn't well yet.

"You're not to blame for this," Georges told her sternly.

Oh, but she was, she thought.

Her eyes were tortured as she turned to him again. "Can't you find a way to get him out of this somehow?" she begged. "Give him a shot, inject him with something that'll bring him around?"

"Maybe the coma's for the best right now. Think of it as being off-line. The body is trying to heal itself," he told her. "Once it does, it'll be on line again." He felt as if their roles had become reversed. The realist had become the optimist and the optimist had fallen victim to pessimism.

Making note of the vital signs and checking them out for himself, Georges did what he could. He could feel Vienna watching his every move. But there was precious little to do. Nothing had changed.

She couldn't continue this way indefinitely, he thought. "Why don't you go home, get some rest? I can have—"

But she was already shaking her head. "I'll rest when he opens his eyes again," she told him fiercely.

There was nothing he could do, short of physically carrying her out. And who knew? Maybe having her here was the best medicine he could prescribe for Amos. So for now, he retreated.

"I'll be back in an hour," he promised.

"Thank you," she murmured without looking up. She continued holding her grandfather's hand, holding on for dear life. Willing him back among the living.

She heard the door closing as Georges slipped out of the cubicle.

"He is right, you know."

Her eyes flew open. Had she just imagined that?

Imagined her grandfather's voice because she wanted to hear it so badly? But his eyes were open and he was looking up at her.

"Oh Grandpa—" Her voice choked and she couldn't get any more out.

She saw his mouth move, but nothing audible came out. Vienna leaned in closer to hear him. But even then, her heart was pounding so hard, it was difficult to make out his words.

Out of nowhere, a feeling slipped over her. Frantic, she pressed the buzzer for the nurse with her other hand. Hard.

"You need to rest," Amos whispered hoarsely against her ear.

She blinked back tears. The feeling inside her grew more ominous. "And you need to get better."

He was struggling with each word. But even so, his thin lips curved in a weak smile. "Even when I am dying, you argue."

"You're not dying," she cried fiercely, but even as she did, she knew it was true. "You hear me? You're not dying, I won't let you."

Georges came rushing in. He'd just passed the nurses' station when he saw the light from Amos's cubicle go off. Fearing the worst, he'd doubled back.

"I…need to…say…this," Amos insisted, each breath audible. "I…love…you. You have been… the…sunshine of…my life…I don't… want…

you…changing." He tried to turn his head and couldn't. But his words were meant for the young man who had come into his life just in time. "Take…take care…of…her for….me…Georges."

"Nobody is going to take care of me but you, Grandpa. You hear me? Only you. Grandpa? Grandpa? Grandpa, please. Don't go," she pleaded. "Don't go."

But Amos's eyes had closed again and he made no answer to her pleas. She felt his fingers go lax in hers.

Vienna's heart broke.

Chapter Fifteen

Once Raul and Zelda had spread the word at the bakery, Vienna had expected that her grandfather's funeral wouldn't be one of those soul-wrenching, solitary affairs where only she and the presiding priest would attend. She'd always known that, no matter where they called home, everyone loved her grandfather. He was just that kind of man.

But she hadn't expected the church and then the cemetery to be overflowing with people the way it was. Every pew in the small church of St. Thomas Aquinas had been filled and people were rubbing elbows at the Peaceful Passage Cemetery.

And, more than that, she really hadn't expected Georges and his entire family, including his sister-in-law-to-be and her daughter and brother. Vienna knew that the other people, the regular customers and their families, had come because of her grandfather. They'd come to pay their respects and to honor a hardworking man who had gladdened the heart of every person his life had touched.

But Georges and especially his family had come because of her. Not because they knew Amos Schwarzwalden and liked him, but because they knew her. And because they felt that she needed the support.

Had Vienna been able to feel, she would have been greatly touched by their gesture and their kindness.

But she couldn't feel. Not anything.

She'd purposely frozen her heart, throwing herself headlong into not just the details of making the funeral arrangements but in running the bakery. She refused to close it after his death, not even for the three days of the wake. She divided her time between the funeral parlor and the bakery, something neither Raul nor Zelda could talk her out of.

The idea behind it all was that she keep moving to outdistance the pain, to dodge and weave and, at all times, to keep several steps ahead of it. If she stood still, if she allowed herself time to think of *anything* but tiny, cluttering details, she knew in her heart that she was going to fall apart.

That was why, even after the funeral, when a large group of the mourners adjourned and followed her from the cemetery to the house she'd shared with her grandfather—the house that was now so very, very empty to her—Vienna did her best to be everywhere. No detail escaped her. None was too large or too small. She made sure that the trays of food found their way to a buffet table and that everyone's glass was always at least halfway filled. She kept an eye on the napkins and the paper plates, making certain that the supply didn't run out.

Though he wanted to help her, Georges had deliberately stood back and watched Vienna at the church, at the cemetery and now here. He knew that he had to give her space. Had to allow her to deal with her grief as she saw fit.

But she wasn't dealing, she was running. He knew the signs. Having done it himself for a number of different reasons, Georges knew the signs well: you didn't stand still long enough for your emotions to catch up and find you. It was the only way to stay invulnerable, to elude the jaws of pain.

But in Vienna's case, the pain *would* come, *would* find her. Most likely when she was least ready for it. And then, then she was going to implode in a million tiny pieces and cave in.

She couldn't continue this shadow dance, Georges decided.

So, as Vienna scooped up an empty tray that had

held an assortment of macadamia chicken and all but aimed her body toward the kitchen in order to replenish the supply, Georges moved directly in front of her, blocking her swift exit.

"I'll get that," he offered. His hand was on the tray, ready to take it from her. But she wouldn't relinquish her hold.

"No," she told him firmly, pulling the tray back. And then, realizing that she'd practically snapped, she added, "Thank you. But no, I have to do it."

He searched her face, looking for an opening. It was as if she'd just dammed up any access to the person inside.

"What you have to do is stop being so stoic," he told her.

She pulled back her lips in a patient smile. It didn't reach her eyes. "There, good Doctor, you're wrong. I *have* to be stoic."

Out of the corner of her eye, she saw Lily coming toward her. She wanted to run, but it was too late. It wasn't that she didn't appreciate what Georges and his family were trying to do, she just didn't want them doing it. Didn't need them doing it. The kinder they tried to be to her, the harder it was to maintain her barriers. And she desperately needed those barriers to keep back all the pain that threatened to find her. To undo her.

Lily's majestic eyebrows narrowed as she took

in what was happening. "Georges, take that tray from her." Her tone left no room for argument.

Vienna held on to the tray as if it were a lifeline. "No, really." She held the tray closer to her. "Please. I *need* to do this."

But Lily was not to be ignored. Very gently, she peeled away Vienna's fingers and physically took the tray away from her. Once in her possession, she thrust the tray to her middle son.

Eyes the color of newly blossoming African violets remained on her. They were filled with compassion and understanding.

"I know," was all she said. "I know." And then, despite the young woman's initial effort to pull away, she enfolded Vienna in her arms.

Realizing that there was no getting around this, that if she resisted, Lily would only continue and that it would draw attention to them, to *her,* Vienna appeared to surrender and allowed herself to be held. Her face buried against Lily's shoulder, Vienna bit her lower lip, trying to keep the walls inside her from crumbling.

Her mind went elsewhere. She forced herself to try to remember how many small sandwiches she'd ordered and then, that failing, she tried to remember all the movements of the last waltz that Strauss had written.

Strauss's compositions had played at the church during the service and then she'd had them piped in over the loudspeaker at the cemetery. Her grandfather had always loved Strauss. Her earliest memories of him were associated with his very old, scratchy record collection. As a gift one Christmas, she'd given him an entire CD collection, meant to replace the old vinyl records. But she caught him playing the latter anyway. He'd said that playing them reminded him of her late grandmother, who'd felt as he did that waltzes were the only melodies worth listening to.

Hearing the notes today had both gladdened her heart and all but torn it in half. At one point, she'd very nearly lost her resolve.

Just as she was in danger of losing it now.

Lily stepped back, releasing her with a resigned sigh. The woman was savvy enough to know that she hadn't accomplished what she'd set out to do. Vienna was still walled in.

"I'm here if you need me," she told Vienna, squeezing her hand.

"That goes for all of us," Georges told her, leaning in as his mother moved away. His eyes held hers for a moment. "Especially me."

Taking the tray back from him, she pressed her lips together and nodded. "I know."

"Do you?" he questioned. She looked at him, confused. It was a simple enough statement that she had uttered. Why was he challenging it? Challenging her? "Do you realize that you're not alone?" he pressed. "That you don't have to be alone?"

Vienna tried her best to smile, to really smile because he knew the difference, but it was a half-hearted effort.

"Oh, but I am," she whispered.

The next moment, she hurried away, to see to the tray, to see to a thousand and one tiny details that mattered to absolutely no one, but the execution of which kept her sane for a minute longer.

It was how she managed to string together her day and all the days that had come between her grandfather's death and now. One scrambling minute after another until an hour faded and then another and another, forming a day.

Vienna leaned against the door, sighing as her eyes fluttered shut for a moment.

It was over.

The people who had attended her grandfather's funeral and the ceremony at the cemetery were finally gone from the house as well. A wave of relief and fear washed over her at the same time. Relief because she no longer had to pretend for anyone that she was all right, and fear for the same reason.

Because she no longer had to pretend.

Because the rest of her life was staring her in the face and she felt so completely, so devastatingly alone. All these years, ever since her parents had died, it had been just her grandfather and her and in her heart, she'd always hoped to expand those numbers. To fall in love, marry, have children and all the while, have her grandfather there as part of the whole.

She wanted him to know how much she appreciated what he had done for her taking care of her all those years. She wanted him to be proud of the way she'd turned out and to know how grateful she was that he had loved her all those years and been there for her whenever she needed him. And sometimes, during her rebellious years, when she'd insisted that she didn't.

Those were the times when she'd needed him most of all, she thought.

Except for now.

Now she needed him. God, but she needed him. Needed something to block all this emptiness dwelling within her. But he was gone.

Busy, get busy, she silently ordered herself. She'd keep busy until she'd drop from exhaustion and fall asleep. It was the only thing that gave her hope.

Feeling like a sleepwalker, Vienna began to pick up the empty paper plates from the table, gathering them from the various surfaces where they had been left.

Janice and Lily had offered to stay and help. She had politely but firmly refused. She wanted to be alone, she'd said.

She'd gotten good at lying, Vienna thought.

"So where would you like me to start?"

A scream escaped her lips as she swung around. The paper plates she'd been holding slipped from her fingers, landing facedown, dirty side against the carpet.

"I guess there," Georges decided, bending down to pick up the plates and the forks she'd dropped.

Vienna pressed her hand over her heart to keep it from breaking out of her chest. It was pounding hard enough to mimic a drumroll.

"What are you doing here?" She could have sworn there was no one in the house. "I thought you'd left with the others."

"Really not all that memorable to you, am I?" he quipped, continuing to gather together the discarded plates. "So much for having an ego." And then he smiled at her, his eyes softening. "I thought you might need some help—"

"I already told your mother no—"

"—and some company." Georges meandered through the living room and the small dining room beyond, stacking plates and cups wherever he found them.

She raised her chin, the lone defender of an abandoned fort. "I said no to that, too."

He paused for a second to pick up a glass that had been left under her grandfather's baby grand piano. "Yes, I know you did."

She circumvented the piano, following him through the room. "So why are you here?"

He placed the stack he'd made on the buffet table. "Because I don't believe you."

She wasn't going to get pulled into a duel of words. Everything was meaningless, anyway. "It doesn't matter what you believe. It's what I want that matters."

Georges turned from what he was doing to look at her. His eyes seemed to hold hers prisoner. "Exactly." His intonation indicated that he was seeing past the barricade of words she'd thrown up and instead, delving into her soul.

Her eyes narrowed. A surge of anger, red-hot and completely out of the blue, with no rhyme nor reason, overtook her. "You're telling me you know my mind better than I do."

If she meant to get into a fight with him, she failed. He looked completely unflappable. "In essence, yes."

Marching over to the front door, she pulled it open, then stood, waiting. "I want you to leave."

He crossed to her, then caught her off guard by slamming the door shut. It vibrated as it settled into its frame. "No, you don't."

"Yes, I do." But when she tried to pull the door open again, he put his hand over hers, preventing her. Her eyes were shooting angry sparks as she looked at him. "Damn it, why are you doing this to me? You know you don't want to be here."

Where the hell had that come from? And then he knew. She was referring to the last time they'd been together, just before she'd discovered her grandfather. But he no longer wanted to swim the waters he'd been testing then. She needed to know that, he thought.

"I've never wanted to be anywhere so much in my life," he contradicted.

No, she wasn't going to believe him. It was a ruse, however well intended, Vienna thought. "You're saying that because you think I'm hurting."

But Georges slowly shook his head. "No, I'm saying that because without you, I'm hurting."

She began to turn away but he caught her by the shoulders, holding her in place. Needing her to listen.

"I won't deny that I wanted to run. That's been the plan all along. Whenever things looked as if they might get serious, I left." She tried to jerk out of his hold, but he only tightened his hands on her shoulders. She needed to hear all of this.

"But a funny thing happened to me on the way to my next escape. I kept putting it off, until I didn't want to go at all." He searched her face to see if she believed him. "You've taken me prisoner and I don't want to leave."

She blew out a breath, wishing he'd let her go. Wishing he'd stop touching her. Her strength ebbed and she needed him to leave before it did. "You've just described the Stockholm syndrome."

He grinned at the mention of that. "I've always wanted to go visit Stockholm," he confessed. "Maybe we can do it together."

"Sorry, too busy." This time, she did manage to break his hold. Turning her back on him, she retreated into the living room.

He kept up, moving faster so that he got ahead of her. "Not if it's a honeymoon. You'd clear time for a honeymoon, wouldn't you?"

He saw her eyes widening in dazed confusion. He had her, he thought.

Georges pretended to consider the matter as if this hadn't already crossed his mind three times over today. "Can't be right now, but we could schedule it for the summer. They take the shackles off me at the hospital in the summer."

"Wait, wait," Vienna pleaded before he could continue, leaving her gasping in the dust. "What honeymoon?"

He looked at her as if he couldn't understand her confusion. "Our honeymoon."

"Our…" Her voice trailed off. She stared at him as if he'd lost his mind. "You can't have a honeymoon unless you're married."

If his grin had been any wider, an extra mouth would have had to be pressed into service to accommodate it. "Exactly."

All right, he was pulling her leg, having fun at her

expense. Vienna crossed her arms before her. "And when did we get married?" she asked sarcastically.

"We didn't." His eyes met hers. His were infinitely warm, teasing. "Yet."

Okay, enough was enough. "Look, if this is some off-the-wall plan to get me to break down and cry because you think I need closure or some such nonsense, it's not going to work."

He stopped her before she reached the kitchen, blocking her way in. "No, it's some off-the-wall plan to get you to say you'll marry me. Does that work?"

Her mouth fell open. "You're asking me to marry you?"

Very slowly, Georges nodded. "Yes."

He didn't mean that—did he? Oh God, did he? "Seriously?"

"Well, I'm smiling," he allowed, then was as serious as he could be, "but yes, seriously."

The next minute, she realized what had to be going on. "Is this a pity proposal? Are you asking me to marry you because you feel sorry for me and this will snap me out of whatever it is you think I have?"

Damn, this woman could come up with more weird road blocks, more excuses to stop him in his tracks than anyone he'd ever known. But then, like Philippe had said, she was a once-in-a-lifetime woman, and women like that were unique in every way.

"The only pity that's involved is if you say no and

then I should be on the receiving end of that pity, not you. But yes, I do want you to snap out of this invulnerable, iron wrap you've spun around yourself." Because otherwise, he was never going to get through to her, he thought.

Georges tried to take her into his arms, but she shrugged his hands away. But he refused to be put off. He'd stood by, gave her her space for these last four days, and that hadn't worked. Now he was doing it his way, the way his heart told him to. And he wasn't about to back off until he'd won her over.

"Your grandfather wouldn't want you to be like this, Vienna. And he wouldn't want you to turn me down." Georges raised his eyebrows, doing his best to look innocent and affable. "He liked me, remember?"

"You're doing this because of Grandpa?" It all suddenly came together for her. "Because he asked you to take care of me."

The look he gave her said she should know better. "I liked that old man a great deal, Vienna, but trust me, I wouldn't marry someone just because a man I admired asked me to. There's such a thing as free will." He let the words sink in before continuing. "And I'm laying down my free will at your feet." He slipped his arms around her. This time, she didn't push him away. It gave him hope. "Marry me, Vienna."

"Why?" she asked. "Give me one good reason why."

Georges didn't say anything for a moment. Instead, he placed his hands on her face, framing it. "Because I love you."

The moment he said them to her, the moment the words penetrated the armor around her heart, Vienna's eyes welled up. The tears she'd been holding back since her grandfather's death, the tears that had gathered in her soul when she believed that she and Georges were through, broke out.

Vienna began to cry. "That's the reason," she whispered.

His hands were still framing her face and he looked intently into her eyes. "Are those tears of joy, or tears of frustration?"

"Will you stop asking me questions?" Vienna raised her mouth to his.

Her lips were so close, he brushed against them as he said, "Just one more." Vienna drew back her head and looked at him, waiting. "Will you marry me? You haven't answered me yet."

"Yes," she cried. "Now shut up and kiss me."

"I can do that."

And he could. And very, very well, too.

* * * * *

Don't miss Marie Ferrarella's next romance,
CAPTURING THE MILLIONAIRE,
available November 2007 from
Silhouette Special Edition.

HARLEQUIN *Romance*®

New York Times bestselling author

DIANA PALMER

Handsome, eligible ranch owner Stuart York knew Ivy Conley was too young for him, so he closed his heart to her and sent her away—despite the fireworks between them. Now, years later, Ivy is determined not to be treated like a little girl anymore…but for some reason, Stuart is always fighting her battles for her. And safe in Stuart's arms makes Ivy feel like a woman…his woman.

Winter Roses

Available November.

COMING NEXT MONTH

#1861 A FAMILY FOR THE HOLIDAYS—Victoria Pade
Montana Mavericks: Striking It Rich

Widow Shandie Solomon moved to Montana with her infant daughter for a new lease on life—and got one, when she opened her beauty parlor next door to Dex Traub's motorcycle shop. By Christmastime the bad boy of Thunder Canyon had Shandie hooked…and she couldn't tell if it was sleigh bells or wedding bells ringing in her future.

#1862 THE SHEIK AND THE CHRISTMAS BRIDE—Susan Mallery
Desert Rogues

Prince As'ad of El Deharia agreed to adopt three orphaned American girls on one condition—that their teacher Kayleen James take over as nanny. In a heartbeat the young ladies turned the playboy prince's household upside down…and Kayleen turned his head. Now he would do anything to keep her—and make her his Christmas bride!

#1863 CAPTURING THE MILLIONAIRE—Marie Ferrarella
The Sons of Lily Moreau

It was a dark and stormy night…when lawyer Alain Dulac crashed his BMW into a tree, and local veterinarian Kayla McKenna came to his aid. Used to rescuing dogs and cats, Kayla didn't know what to make of this strange new animal—but his magnetism was undeniable. Did she have what it took to add this inveterate bachelor to her menagerie?

#1864 DEAR SANTA—Karen Templeton
Guys and Daughters

Investment guru Grant Braeburn had his hands full juggling stock portfolios and his feisty four-year-old daughter, Haley. So the distant widower reluctantly turned to his former wife's flighty best friend Mia Vaccaro for help. Soon Haley's Christmas list included marriage between her daddy and Mia. But would Santa deliver the goods?

#1865 THE PRINCESS AND THE COWBOY—Lois Faye Dyer
The Hunt for Cinderella

Before rancher Justin Hunt settled for a marriage of convenience that would entitle him to inherit a fortune, he went to see the estranged love of his life, Lily Spencer, one more time—and discovered he was a father. Could the owner of Princess Lily's Lingerie and the superrich cowboy overcome their volatile emotions and make love work this time?

#1866 DÉJÀ YOU—Lynda Sandoval
Return to Troublesome Gulch

When a fatal apartment blaze had firefighter Erin DeLuca seeing red over memories of her prom-night car accident that took her fiancé and unborn child years ago, ironically, it was pyrotechnics engineer Nate Walker who comforted her. At least for one night. Now, if only they could make the fireworks last longer…

SSECNM1007